Lila for Gold

by Erin Falligant

American Girl®

For Heide Belz, the goat
whisperer, and Sarah and
her coaching crew at
Madtown Twisters
—E.F.

Table of Contents

Meet the Monettis:
Mom, Jack (he's 8),
me (I'm 10), and Dad

Doing nails with McKenna
when she was my
babysitter

Hanging out at
the gym—Coach
McKenna and Avery,
me, and Emilia

Me and Jack with some of our new friends at horse camp

HONEYCRISP HILL HORSE CAMP

Katie and I have been best friends our whole lives!

Hollyhock is the sweetest horse ever.

Katie's Big News

Chapter 1

N eed a spot?" McKenna called as I mounted the low bar.
I wanted to say no, but jumping to the high bar still
felt a lot safer with my favorite coach spotting, or helping, me.

McKenna smoothed a strand of hair back into her bun
and stepped between me and the high bar. "Ready?" she
asked.

I nodded. Then I cast back, tucked my legs to my chest,
and landed with both feet on the low bar in squat position.
I took a deep breath, prepping for what came next. I
jumped to the high bar, arms outstretched. I felt McKenna's
hand rest briefly on my back. Just as I reached for the high
bar, she let go.

"Nice!" said McKenna, stepping back.

I practiced my tap swing, hollowing out my body as
I swung backward and arching as I swung forward.
Finally, I dropped back down to the mat.

"I don't think you'll need me to spot you for much
longer, do you?" I could hear the smile in McKenna's voice
before I even looked up. Her blue eyes twinkled.

"Maybe not," I said with a grin. I'd come a long way since my fall off the high bar a couple of weeks ago. My fingers had slipped and I'd fallen flat on my back. After that, I got sweaty just *thinking* about jumping to the high bar! But thanks to McKenna, I was back on track.

Next week, at the start of the fall season, I'd find out if I made the Xcel Silver team or Gold. I really wanted Gold, but I didn't have all my skills yet. I still needed a spot for my roundoff back handspring. And I had to land a cart-wheel on the high beam as well as I could on the low beam.

No matter which team I made, I'd be performing in front of real judges at real meets. My stomach somersaulted at the thought. My little brother, Jack, would call that "ner-cited," when you're nervous and excited at the same time. But I was mostly excited. I wanted to do well, earn some medals, and make McKenna proud!

McKenna was my babysitter when she first moved from Seattle to Saint Paul for college three years ago. This year, she's coaching gymnastics at Aberg's Gym instead of competing on her college team. When she asked if I wanted to join the competitive program at Aberg's, I said yes!

McKenna handed me my water bottle and gestured toward the beams, where my teammates were warming up. Tall, redheaded Avery Thomas was practicing a handstand, her legs extended perfectly straight over her shoulders.

She was so strong! Avery had been on Gold for a year and would move up to Platinum someday soon.

Emilia Ramos was practicing full turns on one foot. When she pivoted toward me, she caught my eye and waved—and then wobbled, her brown eyes wide. She swung her arms around, trying to keep her balance. Finally, she leaped sideways off the beam and fell to the floor laughing. Nobody plays up their wipeouts quite as much as Emilia. I think she'll be a famous actor someday.

When I reached the beam, Emilia was straddling it, her long, dark braid draped over her shoulder. "You look like you're riding a horse," I joked.

She grinned and reached for imaginary reins, holding her hands the way we'd learned at horse camp over the summer. "Did you get your invitation to Fall Fest at Honeycrisp Hill?" she asked. "It's in October. You'll get to see Hollyhock!"

"I did," I said. "I can't wait!" I hadn't seen my favorite horse since camp ended a week ago. "I get to see her next Saturday too, when Jack goes for his riding lesson."

As I mounted the beam, I imagined I was swinging my leg over Hollyhock's back. I could almost smell her sweet horsey scent.

Emilia said, "I bet she misses you. I mean, you did kind of save her."

Emilia exaggerates sometimes, but she was sort of right about this. Hollyhock had spooked around dogs and almost got sent away from camp. Mr. Benson, the camp owner, let me help train her to get her over her fear. But riding Hollyhock had helped *me* get over my fear of falling off the high bar too. So I figured we were even.

"All right, girls," said McKenna as she sat on a bench by the beams. "How about if we focus on acro skills tonight? Cartwheels, handstands, and back walkovers."

When Emilia groaned quietly, I gave her a sympathetic smile. She'd been working on her back walkovers, and I knew they kind of freaked her out. "Let's move to the low beam," I whispered. "I need to practice my cartwheels there anyway."

"You're the best," Emilia whispered back.

Emilia and I were friends—finally! But I still missed Katie, my best friend. We've known each other our whole lives, and we started doing gymnastics together when we were six. Katie wasn't sure she wanted to join competitive gymnastics, so when I came to Aberg's, she stayed at our old gym.

She wasn't at horse camp either, which meant we'd spent a lot of time apart over the summer.

Now school was starting again, and Katie and I would be in the same fifth-grade class. Plus, we had a sleepover planned for tomorrow. A sleepover on Labor Day weekend is one of our favorite traditions. We'd do fun hairstyles, shop for matching school supplies, eat chocolate-chip pancakes, play with her cat, Harry . . .

Just thinking about the weekend gave me a boost of courage. I lunged into my cartwheel, kicked my legs up into a straddle handstand, and landed back on the beam without even the slightest wobble.

"Nice, Lila!" Avery called from the high beam.

Emilia raised her eyebrows in surprise. Avery had been my toughest critic over the summer, always telling me what I was doing wrong. When I finally asked her to start telling me what I was doing *right* instead, things got a whole lot better. And a compliment from an athlete like Avery was a pretty big deal.

"Thanks," I said, feeling a flutter of pride.

"You need to do that on the high beam now," Avery reminded me.

And just like that, she brought me back down to earth. I was getting better, but I still had a long way to go. So I stopped thinking about chocolate-chip pancakes and tried to focus. I hadn't made the Gold team *yet*.

"Knock, knock!" My eight-year-old brother burst through my bedroom door just as I finished packing for my sleepover with Katie.

Jack never actually knocks before coming into my room, but knock-knock jokes are his new favorite thing. When I saw the joke book in his hand, I knew I was in trouble.

"Who's there?" I said with a sigh.

"Just a sec." Jack had lost his place in the book. He flipped a few pages and then his face brightened. "Okay, weekend—that's who."

"Weekend who?" I asked.

"Weekend do anything we want!" he announced. "Get it?" Before I could answer, he jumped onto my bed. "So what should we do?"

"Sorry," I said, zipping up my backpack. "I'm going to Katie's for the night."

Jack's face fell. "Okay, just one more joke." He opened his book.

"No, I'm going to be late," I said. "Tell them to Mom instead. She just got home from the hospital."

Mom must have heard, because she poked her head into the room. She was wearing blue scrubs, and her eyes looked tired. Mom works as a nurse at a children's hospital, and sometimes she has to work twelve hours straight. "Tell me what?" she asked.

"Knock, knock," said Jack.

Mom laughed. "We'd better say goodbye now," she said, giving me a hug. "There are a lot of jokes in that book."

I made my escape just as Mom said, "Who's there?"

I raced down the porch steps and toward the garden shed to get my bike. "Give my best to Harry!" Dad called from the backyard, where he was trimming trees. He meant Katie's cat. Dad is as much of an animal lover as Jack, but they're both allergic to cats.

"I'll tell him you say hello!" I joked as I fastened my helmet.

"And remember to text me when you get there," Dad called as I pedaled down the driveway. I waved to let him know I would.

Katie lives five blocks from me in a part of Saint Paul, Minnesota, where all the houses are a hundred years old and the trees are even older. They arch over the street like a tunnel. I biked past wrought iron gates and lampposts. Past Victorian-style houses with wraparound porches and turrets jutting out of their rooftops. Past the park where Katie and I meet to hang out or practice gymnastics.

When I reached Katie's block, a black and white blur burst out of the bushes.

"Harry!"

The cat started to slink, as if he knew he'd been busted.

Katie named him after Harry Houdini, the great escape artist. Even though Harry is supposed to stay inside, he's good at slipping through the door and escaping. But Katie knows how to bring him back.

"Harry!" she called from her porch. "Tuna!" At the crack of the can lid, Harry shot back toward the house.

"Gotcha!" Katie cried.

By the time I parked my bike, Harry was in her arms, looking limp and defeated. A morsel of tuna was stuck to his nose.

"Oh, Harry," I said, shaking my head. "Did we ruin your big adventure?"

Katie answered for him in her raspy little Harry voice: "You never let me have any fun." Then she wiggled her head, her dark, shiny braids spinning side to side. "See what I did?"

"French-braid Friday!" I announced. It's another one of our favorite traditions.

"You do them better, though," said Katie. "C'mon!"

I followed her into the house, waving to her mom, who was working in her home office. "Hi, Mrs. Gundersen!" She's a professor at the University of Minnesota.

"Lila!" she called back. "Good to see you. Help yourself to the cookies on the counter."

I scooped up a handful of molasses cookies and followed Katie to her bedroom. The walls, which used to be blue, were now a bright shade of purple. "When did you paint your room?" I asked, nearly choking on my cookie.

Katie shrugged. "A few weeks ago," she said. "You haven't been here since before horse camp, remember?"

I felt a twinge of guilt. I had been at horse camp during the day and doing gymnastics at night, so Katie and I hadn't spent as much time together as usual. Seeing a new color on her walls reminded me that we'd fallen out of step as best friends. But we were back to normal now—mostly.

Katie plunked Harry down in a doll bed. Instead of escaping, he curled up and went right to sleep. Then Katie whirled around to face me.

"I have news," she said. "Really *big* news."

"You painted your room purple?" I joked.

"No," she said. "You'd better sit down for this."

"O-kay," I said, sitting on the bed. My stomach twisted. Was Katie moving or something?

"I'm joining the gym," she blurted.

I felt my jaw drop open. "*My* gym?" I said. "Aberg's?"

She nodded so hard, her braids bounced.

"When?"

"Tuesday."

For a moment, we were silent. Then I let out a whoop and launched at Katie, wrapping her up in a giant hug.

She pulled back laughing. "Stop!" she cried. "You're choking me!"

I let go. But when Harry meowed, scolding us for making so much noise, we burst out laughing again.

Katie and I flopped down on her bed, and all sorts of questions raced through my mind. "I thought you didn't want to join a competitive program," I said.

Katie shrugged. "I miss you, so I'm going to give it a try."

"Aw," I said. "I miss you too! But don't you have dance lessons Saturday mornings?"

"Yes, but I'll only go to Aberg's on Tuesdays and Thursdays," Katie explained. "McKenna said that would be okay."

At the mention of my coach's name, everything started feeling real. "So on Tuesday, we won't just be going to fifth grade together," I said slowly. "We'll also be going to the same gym together after school?"

"Yep," said Katie with a grin. "Things will be just like they were before."

I was so happy, I thought my heart might explode. "I'm gonna need another hug," I warned Katie. "Incoming!"

She shrieked and squirmed away, but I held on tight. As we toppled to the floor, laughing, Harry bolted out of the room.

Ready to Work

Chapter 2

R eady to work?" asked McKenna.

We were at the gym Tuesday night, and I still couldn't believe Katie was there with me.

"Ready to fly!" my teammates and I answered. Katie looked at us as if we were speaking a foreign language.

"It's how we start every practice," I whispered.

Katie nibbled on her fingernail, taking in the sights and sounds of Aberg's Gym, which was bigger than our old gym. I was used to the commotion—the slap of feet hitting the mat, the squeak of the springboard on vault, the voices and laughter of the coaches and girls scattered around the gym. Mats covered the floor like giant puzzle pieces. Trophies and posters lined the walls. Aberg's had way more beams, bars, and vault tables than our old gym.

I was relieved that Katie wasn't the only new girl. A tiny blond girl about Jack's age stood with us. There was a new assistant coach too, a teenage girl named Sawyer.

When McKenna led us toward the mats, Katie and I plopped down next to each other. Emilia waved at Katie.

"Hey, I met you at the riding demo at horse camp!"

Katie had come to watch me ride on the last day of camp, and she had met Emilia then too. "Lila braided your hair that day," Katie said with a smile. "I remember."

"All right, girls," said McKenna, calling us to attention. "We have two new gymnasts on Silver this fall. Welcome, Grace"—she smiled at the blond girl—"and welcome, Katie." McKenna winked at Katie. They already knew each other from back when McKenna used to babysit me. "Avery and Emilia will be competing on Gold. And Lila . . ."

I held my breath.

"Lila is going for Gold," said McKenna, "but she's not quite there yet."

My stomach sank. I'd worked so hard! But McKenna didn't think I was ready. I stared down at my hands.

McKenna caught my eye and gave me a reassuring smile. "Here's what I propose," she said. "We have a mock meet on October fifth. It's like a practice meet before competition season starts in November. Let's have you compete on Gold at the mock meet, and if you do well, we'll officially move you up to the Gold team."

My chest flooded with relief. "That sounds great!" I said. McKenna was giving me more time! I was going to practice harder than ever and rock that mock meet.

Katie squeezed my hand. She knew how much I wanted Gold.

McKenna handed us forms we could use to rank music for our floor routines. "We get to choose our own song?" I asked.

"Gold gymnasts do," said McKenna. "Check out the website on that form. Then let me know your top three choices by next Tuesday, okay?"

"Don't pick anything that's really popular," Avery added. "You'll be using this song for a couple of years, and you don't want to get sick of it." Avery already had her music from last year. I'd seen her practicing her floor routine to it.

Katie's form didn't have a website listed, but it had a couple of song choices. "Ooh, I love this one!" she said, pointing to a song called "Take a Chance." "My mom and I know every word." She was so excited, her knee started bouncing.

I felt bouncy too. I still had a chance at making Gold, and Katie and I were together at the gym again. Having Katie by my side made *everything* more fun. During hand-stand practice, when we were walking on our hands, Avery kept giving Grace and Katie tips. "Remember to point your toes, Grace!" she said. "Squeeze your legs tight, Katie. Squeeze everything—your abs and butt too."

Katie waited until we were both upside down. Then she whispered in her raspy little Harry-the-cat voice, "Lila, are you squeezing your butt?"

I immediately toppled to the floor giggling.

Avery, who was walking on her hands in a complete circle, lowered her legs and shot me a look.

I held my breath, trying to stop laughing. But as soon as Avery turned away, Katie pointed to her rear and whispered, "Squeeeeeeeeeze."

I buried my face in my hands. Now I was laughing so hard, my stomach hurt. Which meant I couldn't squeeze my abs. Which meant I couldn't walk on my hands.

McKenna squatted beside us. "Try to pull it together, girls," she gently scolded. By then, I was crying. Katie is the *only* person in the whole world who can make me laugh so hard, I cry.

"Let's move you two over to the wall," said McKenna, waving us away from the other girls. "You won't distract anyone over there." We followed her, still giggling, and when McKenna left us by the wall, I could see that she was laughing too.

Katie's laughter is contagious like that. Even Emilia started giggling! But Avery is all business, all the time, at the gym. She wasn't even smiling.

Right then and there, I knew. Katie and Emilia weren't just going to be teammates. They were going to be friends. But Katie and Avery? Not a chance.

On Saturday, when Dad pulled into the gravel driveway at Honeycrisp Hill, I started cheering. I looked uphill, past the riding arena, toward the horse paddocks and barn. Hollyhock was up there somewhere, waiting for me.

Katie cheered too. We were in the back seat, with Jack squeezed in between us. He covered his ears. "Not so loud!"

But I couldn't help it. It was a sunny afternoon, I had my best friend with me, and we were about to see my favorite horse.

"Do you think Hollyhock will remember me?" I worried out loud.

Katie reached across Jack and slapped my knee. "Of course she will!" she said. "Animals are smart—and loyal."

I hoped Katie was right.

As soon as Dad parked the car, Jack climbed over me and out the door. I knew who he was looking for—Mighty Mae, the camp corgi. The squat little dog with big ears was right there, ready to greet him.

"Oh, she's so cute!" cried Katie.

Mighty Mae gave Jack a proper face licking. "Stop!" he cried, laughing. But I knew he loved it.

Katie squatted to hug Mighty Mae, burying her face in the dog's golden fur. "I can't do this with Harry," Katie said, her voice muffled.

"Harry doesn't appreciate hugs."

When Freya, a camp counselor, called hello to us from the goat pen, we all raced over to say hi.

"Are you ready for your lesson?" Freya asked Jack. "Mr. Benson has Joker saddled up." She gestured toward the arena, where a black pony was munching on grass. Mr. Benson, a bearded man in a flannel shirt, waved to us.

Jack's face fell a little. "Isn't Luke giving me my lesson?" he asked. Luke was Mr. Benson's grandson—and Jack's favorite counselor.

"He left for college a few days ago," said Freya. "I'm sorry, buddy. But he'll be back for Fall Fest. You can see him then."

At that Jack perked up and jogged over to Joker.

I reached down to pet the goats. I saw that one had a very round belly. "I don't remember this one," I said.

"That's Gretta," said Freya. "She's going to be a mama very soon."

Katie sucked in her breath. "Baby goats?"

"Any day now," Freya promised. "But first things first." She glanced at me, her eyes sparkling. "I told Hollyhock you were coming. Want to go say hi?"

My feet were moving before she'd even finished the question.

"Wait up!" cried Katie. "I want to see Hollyhock, too."

I raced past the goat pen, through the grassy pasture, and across the gravel drive toward the horse paddocks.

Hollyhock shared a small paddock with her buddy, Dakota—at least she did the last time I had seen her. But when I reached the enclosure, it was empty. My stomach dropped. "Where is she?" I cried.

Katie stopped beside me, panting. "She's here somewhere. Freya said so!"

I jogged over to the larger paddock that held the mares, and then I saw her. Standing in a corner, close to a black and white paint horse, stood my beautiful palomino. Her golden coat shimmered in the afternoon sunlight.

"She's in with the full herd," I said to Katie. "They've accepted her!"

I tried to explain what that meant. "Hollyhock was new to the herd this summer. I think that's why I bonded with her—because I was the new girl too, at the gym. And it takes time for a herd to accept a new horse, so Hollyhock spent most of her time with her buddy, Dakota." I pointed toward the paint horse. "Mr. Benson said having a buddy makes it easier to join the herd."

Katie sighed. "I'm the new girl at the gym now," she said. "But at least I have a buddy there too." She grinned at me.

"You do," I said. "C'mon. Let's say hi to Hollyhock!"

I walked slowly toward Hollyhock, hoping she'd

remember me—that things would feel the same. "Hey, girl," I called as we got closer.

Hollyhock pricked her ears and lifted her head. Dakota did too, and then went right back to eating hay. When Hollyhock started walking toward the fence, my heart leaped in my chest.

"See?" whispered Katie. "She *does* remember you!"

Hollyhock greeted me with a nicker and blew a warm puff of air onto my outstretched hand. When she was close enough, I patted her neck. Then I reached up to stroke the white blaze on her forehead, just under her forelock. She closed her eyes a little, letting me know that I was scratching her favorite spot.

When she nuzzled me for more, I kissed the top of her velvety nose and breathed in her sweet hay smell. And just like that, it was as if no time had passed. She was still my Hollyhock.

"You can pet her," I said to Katie, who was hanging back a little.

Katie approached slowly. "She's so big," she said, stroking Hollyhock.

"But she's gentle," I reassured Katie.

"And she loves to be groomed," called Freya as she crossed the gravel drive.

"Yes!" I said excitedly. Freya knows how much I love doing horse hairstyles.

Freya let me lead Hollyhock to the barn. She walked right beside me, her head bobbing, all the way into the grooming stall. Freya brought us a pink bin with brushes and combs, and then she reminded us about safety.

"Be careful when you're walking behind Hollyhock," she warned Katie. "Keep a hand on her rump so she knows where you are. And watch where you put your feet. If you stand too close, she might accidentally step on you."

Katie looked down at her feet.

"That's why we wear riding boots," I explained.

While I used a soft brush to make Hollyhock's coat shiny, Katie brushed her other side.

"Hollyhock is in heaven," I said. "She loves this."

Katie cocked her head. "How can you tell?"

I pointed to Hollyhock's eyes. "See how she kind of closes her eyes? That means she's relaxed. Or her bottom lip might droop. Or she might lean into you and give you a horse hug. That's how you know she's happy."

"Huh," said Katie. "I didn't know all that. I guess I don't speak horse. I speak dog, and definitely cat, and a little Spanish. But no horse."

I laughed. "I'm still learning horse language too. But Hollyhock has taught me a lot."

When I was done brushing, I braided Hollyhock's tail. Katie started braiding Hollyhock's mane. Then, way too

soon, I heard Jack and Mr. Benson talking as they led Joker back to his stall.

"No, stay *in* your stall, Joker," Jack scolded the pony, who wasn't always the best listener.

Then *clang!* A stall door slammed shut. Hollyhock snorted and stepped sideways—right onto my foot!

"Ouch!" I cried, trying to keep my voice down so I wouldn't scare her even more. But, wow, did that hurt. Tears sprang to my eyes.

I limped out of the stall and sat down, trying to get my boot off.

"Are you okay?" asked Freya. She ushered Katie out of the stall and shut the door, then helped me peel off my sock. "Oh, she got you good."

My baby toe was already swollen and turning a blotchy pink. "She didn't mean to!" I said right away. I didn't want Hollyhock to get in trouble.

"I know," said Freya. "We all spooked at that sound."

Jack poked his head out of Joker's stall. "Sorry!" he said. "I didn't close the door all the way and Joker tried to get out. Did you hurt your foot?"

When Mr. Benson heard that, he hurried out of the stall. "Let me see," he said, pulling his glasses from his pocket. He held up my foot for a closer look. "Good thing you were wearing your boots. But you're going to have a pretty sore, bruised toe. You might need to stay off it for a week or so."

"For a *week*?" I squawked.

Katie gave me a wide-eyed sympathetic look. Then she turned to Mr. Benson. "I've never seen Lila sit still for a whole week."

I had a mock meet in four weeks—a meet that would decide whether I made the Gold team. I couldn't stay off my foot for a week. I had too many skills to learn!

But now my toe was throbbing, telling me that I might not have a choice.

Team Purple

Chapter 3

uesday morning, I rolled out of bed fast—too fast. When I hit the footboard of my bed, my little toe burned with pain. Was it ever going to heal? When I'd gotten back from Honeycrisp Hill, Mom had taped the toe to the one next to it for support. I'd been icing it since Saturday, and had been careful not to put too much weight on it. It didn't hurt as much now, and it wasn't pink anymore. But it had turned a raging shade of purple.

Once the pain eased up, I half ran, half limped to the kitchen. "Mom!" I cried. "It's Tuesday. Can I go?"

She turned from the counter, a grapefruit in one hand and a knife in the other. "Go where?"

"Gymnastics!" I said. "Will you look at my toe?" I propped up my foot on the table.

"Gross," said Jack. "Trying to eat here." He slid his cereal bowl as far away from my purple toe as he could.

"Sorry." I lowered my foot, and Mom squatted next to it. She went straight into nurse mode, wiggling my toe and comparing it to the same toe on my other foot. "It's less swollen now," she said. "Does it still hurt?"

I shrugged. "Only sometimes."

"Then, yes, you may go to practice—"

"Yes!" I pumped my fist in the air.

"—*if* you take it easy," Mom finished. She dipped her chin and gave me a stern look to be sure I was listening.

"I will," I promised. Then I raced back to my bedroom to get dressed for school. I could hardly wait to tell Katie.

"That's purple, all right," Katie said, staring at my toe.

We were sitting in her bedroom after school, trying to make my injured toe less noticeable.

"I told you!" I cried.

Katie grinned. "Luckily for you, purple is my favorite color."

"Since when?" I asked. "You've always loved blue."

She gestured toward her purple walls. "A girl is allowed to change her mind. And purple is going to be *your* new favorite color too—wait and see."

Katie pulled out a bin of nail polish from under her bed. She rummaged through it until she found a bottle of violet polish. When she held it next to my toe, she nodded with satisfaction. "Yep, this is the perfect shade." She pretended to read the name of the polish on the label. "This is called 'Bruised Toe.'"

"That is *not* what it's called," I said, laughing.

"Okay, sit still!" she said as she uncapped the bottle. "I don't want to spill it."

The instant Katie set the bottle on the floor, a paw snaked out from under the bed and tried to snatch it.

"Harry, no!" cried Katie, swatting the paw away. "That's not for you. It's not your color."

A defiant *mew* sounded from under the bed.

Katie started polishing my big toe, which tickled. But I tried to sit perfectly still. When she got to my pinky toe, she started getting sloppy.

"Katie, you're totally missing my nail," I said. "Wipe that off!"

"I *meant* to do that," she insisted. "If everyone's looking at your messy polish, they won't even notice your toe. See what I mean?"

She sat back so that I could take a look. Sure enough, the purple polish made my bruised toe a lot less noticeable. "Katie," I said, "you're a genius."

She shrugged. "That's what they say," she joked. "I'm going to put some on too. I love this color. Go, Team Purple!"

By the time we walked into Aberg's Gym, Katie and I were full-on Team Purple. We were wearing purple polish on our toes, purple ribbons in our hair, and matching purple leotards.

When one of the older girls on the Platinum team complimented our outfits, I grinned at Katie. Somehow my best friend could make even a bruised toe feel fun.

As we hung our backpacks on hooks, Emilia bounded over. "Hey, I like what's going on here!" she said, circling her hand in front of us. "Is it Purple Tuesday?"

"Yes!" said Katie, her eyes flashing. "Purple Tuesday. That could be a new tradition."

When McKenna called us to the mats, I fished my floor music form out of my backpack. I had chosen three songs: a country one that Dad and I sing at the top of our lungs whenever we hear it, a tune from a musical Mom and I saw last spring, and a cartoon theme song.

As soon as Katie and I sat down, Avery's eyes flickered toward our painted nails. "You can't wear nail polish at meets," she pointed out. "That's a rule at Aberg's."

Katie pursed her lips. She cast Emilia a sideways glance, and Emilia rolled her eyes knowingly.

"Well, that's boring," said Katie, more to me than to Avery.

McKenna smiled. "It's true that we don't allow you to wear polish at meets," she said gently, "but this isn't a meet. This is practice. And I think that's a lovely shade of purple."

Katie leaned sideways to give McKenna an impulsive hug. "Thank you," said Katie. "I think so too."

When McKenna and Sawyer started warm-ups, Katie whispered to me, "Is Avery always on the lookout for mistakes?"

I nodded. "She notices everything," I whispered back.

"Well, she didn't notice your toe yet," Katie said. "Score a point for Team Purple."

I giggled, but as soon as we moved to the vault, *I* noticed my toe. It was not happy.

I couldn't sprint down the runway to the vault, so I jogged instead. I stepped onto the springboard instead of jumping onto it. And I did a lousy roundoff over the vault table before landing in the foam pit.

When we moved to floor, Avery caught up to me. "Do you have a side ache or something?" she asked.

"What do you mean?"

"You weren't running very fast on vault."

I shrugged. "I'm just a little off today," I said.

I tried to baby my toe while we worked on tumbling. I couldn't do the roundoff part of my roundoff back hand-spring, because sprinting across the mat hurt too much! But Katie was feeling no pain. I watched her whip off a front handspring to a roundoff. I'd forgotten how much air she could get. She had springs in her feet.

"Looking good, Katie," said McKenna. "You're bouncy today!"

"Thanks," said Katie, her cheeks pink. She jogged over

to me. "Does it hurt?" she whispered, her eyes darting toward my toe.

I nodded. "Hopefully it'll feel better on beam."

But it didn't. Every time I tried to go up on my tiptoes, my toe hurt. And I couldn't wrap my foot around the beam for balance. Even with nine toes hanging on for dear life, I wobbled so much that I finally gave up. *Take a water break,* I told myself with a sigh.

I was in such a hurry to get off the beam that I did a roundoff dismount out of habit—and came down hard on my toe.

Smack!

The pain shot up my foot and brought me to the ground.

Emilia leaped off her beam to squat beside me. When she saw my toe, she gasped. "It's already purple!" she squawked. "Oh this is bad—really, really bad. My ankle swelled up like that when I broke it last year."

"Shh!" I whispered, hoping no one had heard. I caught Katie's eye and mouthed, *Help!*

Katie's eyes widened. She glanced at McKenna, who was working with Grace on her handstand. But now Avery was peering down at me. "You *broke* your *toe*?" she said. "That could take two months to heal."

At the words *broke* and *toe*, McKenna was suddenly by my side. "What happened?" she said, her brow furrowed with concern. "Let me see."

"I didn't break it!" I said quickly. "It's just bruised. Hollyhock stepped on it Saturday at horse camp."

McKenna sucked in her breath. "I know how that feels. I got stepped on by a horse once. Why didn't you tell me your toe was hurting?"

I shrugged. "I didn't want to have to sit out practice. The mock meet is only like three weeks away!"

"You were lucky," McKenna said. "Hiding even a small injury can lead to big trouble. I wish you had told me." She led me to the bench. "Sit tight for a second. I'm going to tape up that toe."

When McKenna got back, she held up three rolls of athletic tape—blue, red, and purple. "Which one?"

"Purple," I said with a grin. "Definitely purple."

"All right," she said, sitting on the mat. "We'll tape your pinky toe to the one next to it. It's called 'buddy taping.' That'll give it more stability and help it hurt less."

"So I can practice?" I asked.

McKenna bit her lip and shook her head. "No," she said. "You should probably sit out this week until that toe feels better. But we can have you work on strength and flexibility exercises that'll keep you moving forward on your skills. Sound good?"

The voice in my head hollered, *No! That sounds terrible! I can't lose a week of practice!* Instead, I nodded.

As I sat on the mat doing stretches, panic rose in my

chest, especially when McKenna said she wanted to meet with us one-on-one this week to teach us our personalized floor routines. "Lila, you and I will wait until next week to give your toe time to heal," she added gently.

Katie gave me her sad puppy face. She always knows just how I'm feeling. "It'll get better," she promised me.

But would it get better in time? I was losing a whole week! How was I supposed to learn my floor routine, get my Gold skills, and practice enough to rock the mock meet in such a short time?

I looked down at my taped toes. I was going to need more than a little buddy tape to pull this off. I was going to need a miracle.

By Thursday afternoon, the leaves outside Aberg's Gym were turning yellow—and my bruised toe was too. It didn't hurt as much anymore, but watching my teammates practice without me stung. I was doing handstands against the wall, feeling like my whole world had turned upside down.

Katie was humming the music for her floor routine, which McKenna had taught her the night before. When Katie pulled up the song on her phone, she busted a few dance moves right there on the mat. "C'mon," she said, holding out her hand to Emilia. "Dance with me!"

Emilia jumped up and joined the dance party. When

the music ended, they struck dramatic poses and then collapsed into giggles.

McKenna applauded. "I give you both perfect tens for creativity," she said with a smile. "Now let's see your actual routine, Katie. Do you remember the moves?"

Katie nodded, her cheeks pink. She handed McKenna her phone, and when the music started, she launched into the routine—stopping now and then to look to McKenna for reminders.

When the music ended, Emilia held up nine fingers. "9.9!" she declared.

Katie grinned. "Not a perfect 10?" she joked.

"No," Avery piped up. "Your legs have to be even in your split leaps. Your front leg was higher than your back leg."

Katie's face fell. "Seriously?" she said.

Avery nodded. "It helps if you practice leaps with alternating legs—first with your right leg in front and then with your left."

Katie shot me a look that said, *Is this girl for real?* I lowered myself out of my handstand, knowing whatever happened next wasn't going to be good.

McKenna swooped in to smooth things over. "Katie, I'm amazed at how much of your routine you've already memorized. Nice work! And Avery, an alternating leg drill is a great idea. How about if we all try it?"

Katie set her jaw with determination as she leaped down the mat, alternating between right leg leaps and left leg leaps. When it was time for a water break, she headed straight for me.

"Was Avery really judging my floor routine the very first day I practiced it?" she whisper-spat.

I sighed. "Kind of." I knew how it felt to have Avery hovering nearby, giving a few too many tips. "You did rock that alternating leg drill though," I said brightly. "Your legs were *definitely* more even by the end of that!"

Katie glowered at me. "So you're saying I needed to work on my split leaps?"

My stomach clenched. "No," I said quickly. "I thought your routine looked really good."

Katie forced a smile and then jogged back toward the water fountain, where Emilia was waiting.

Now missing practice because of a bruised toe wasn't the only thing I was worried about. Katie's feelings were bruised too. Would she and Avery *ever* get along?

Avery's Advice

Chapter 4

When Mom dropped me off at Aberg's Monday night, I hurried through the lobby and pulled open the door to the gym. The first thing I noticed was how *quiet* the gym was now that regular practice had ended. No voices. No feet hitting the mats. No sound at all.

McKenna sat cross-legged on the mat. "Hey!" she said, hopping to her feet. "How's that toe?"

"Better," I said. My bruise had turned from yellow to brown. It still hurt a little, but I needed to get back to work. The mock meet was less than three weeks away. I was running out of time!

McKenna pulled up a video on her phone, and the country song I'd chosen wafted out.

"I get my first choice?" I said.

"Yep," said McKenna. "I think it'll work well."

I started humming as I pulled off my sweats. "It's going to be hard not to sing along," I confessed.

McKenna laughed. "So sing!" she said. "Have fun with it."

"Katie would like that idea," I said.

McKenna smiled. "I can tell you two like being at the same gym again," she said.

I nodded. "It's great, but . . . I'm not sure Katie was ready for how serious things, or gymnasts—like Avery—can get."

McKenna tilted her head. "Avery and Katie definitely have different approaches to gymnastics, but that's okay. Different personalities make for a more balanced team, don't you think?"

I nodded again, but I wasn't so sure our team was balanced yet.

"And now," McKenna said dramatically, "let me show you the routine I put together for *you*."

She started the video over and handed me her phone. There was McKenna, performing my routine. She didn't do all the tumbling moves, but she showed off the dance parts. She looked so graceful! I could tell she'd been doing gymnastics for a long time.

"That looks really fun," I said after the song ended. "I hope I can remember it all."

"We'll learn it in chunks," she said. "Ready?"

I stood in the corner of the mat, and she showed me the first few moves. "When the song starts, you'll turn on the ball of your foot like this, hands on hips. Now touch your shoulders, extend your arms, and dance to the other corner."

I practiced that a few times, and then McKenna asked, "What do you want to do for your first tumbling pass? Roundoff back handspring?"

I swallowed hard and nodded. "I don't have it yet, though. I still need a spot."

"We'll get there," she said. "Want to try one now?"

I hesitated. I wasn't sure about my toe. "Maybe just the back handspring part," I said.

McKenna spotted me, one hand behind my back, as I squatted with my arms at my sides. Then I pushed off the ground, throwing my arms upward and arching my back. As soon as my hands touched the ground behind me, I tried to drive my feet and legs over my head.

"Snap your feet to the ground," McKenna reminded me. But I had no snap! She had to help me flip my legs over my head. When my toe hit the ground, I was relieved that it didn't hurt. It stung my pride, though. I sighed with frustration. Would I *ever* get a back handspring?

McKenna squeezed my shoulder. "We'll keep working on that one," she said. "Let's focus on your choreography tonight, okay? For the second dance pass, I was thinking you could do a front walkover and land in a sit. That'll show off your flexibility. Want to try it?"

I nodded. A front walkover I could do. If only back handsprings were that easy!

Then she showed me the leap pass. "You rock your leaps

and jumps," she said. "Flexibility helps you with those too."

After McKenna taught me each part of my routine, we ran through the whole thing again—twice. "What do you think?" she asked.

"I love it," I said, giving McKenna a quick hug. I didn't love the fact that I couldn't do a roundoff back handspring yet. But I loved knowing I could *finally* start practicing my routine.

When I ran out the front door to where Mom was parked, my toe didn't hurt at all.

"One week till the meet," I whispered to myself.

It was Saturday morning at the gym, which meant Katie was at dance lessons. Saturday mornings without Katie felt way different from Tuesdays and Thursdays. They were never as much fun, but I tried to focus on my routines and do my best.

Except my best wasn't good enough yet! At least not when it came to back handsprings. I could do them on the trampoline, but I still couldn't do them on the floor without a spot.

"What if I need a spot at the mock meet?" I asked McKenna after another failed attempt.

"Then I'll spot you," she said. *And I'll bump you down to the Silver team.* She didn't actually say that last part, but the

voice in my head did. I went into beam practice with that
worry hanging over me.

After warming up, I tried my full beam routine, naming
the skills in my head so I wouldn't forget. *Handstand, step,
knee up, T with arms . . .*

When it was time for my cartwheel, I held my breath—
even though McKenna always reminds us not to. *Pretend
you're on the low beam,* I told myself. Except the ground was
so far away!

I lunged forward, kicking my legs overhead. When my
feet landed back on the beam, I immediately lost my balance
and started flailing my arms, just like Emilia does. But I
gripped the beam with all ten toes. I held on and didn't fall.

"There you go, Lila," called Sawyer. "Keep going."

I did—trying to focus on
my split jump. But I kept thinking about that cartwheel. If I
couldn't do it on the high beam
yet, how was I going to pull it
off at the mock meet in only
seven days?

I looked around the gym
again, wishing Katie were here.
She wasn't, but Avery was,
doing a perfect back walkover
on the high beam.

So I took a deep breath and did something I almost never do: I asked Avery for advice on my cartwheel.

Avery's face lit up like it was the best day ever. "Try going slower," she said. "And really grab the beam with your fingers. Don't just set your hands on top."

I took Avery's advice and tried my cartwheel again, gripping the beam tightly and slowing down each move. I still wobbled on my landing, but I felt stronger, especially when Avery said, "That's better."

"*Much* better," Emilia added from the beam next to us. "Go, Lila. Go Lila." She launched into a cheer routine, then promptly fell off the beam.

By the time we moved to bars, I was laughing with Emilia and still floating from Avery's compliment. When I mounted the low bar, I didn't ask for a spot. "You've got this, Lila!" McKenna called.

Somehow, I knew I did. I cast back. Then I did a couple of hip circles, swinging my whole body under the bar and bringing it back up and over.

I felt strong, ready for what was coming next. *You've got this*, I reminded myself as I cast back once more. I tucked my legs and landed in the squat position on the low bar. Then I took a deep breath, set my sights on the high bar, and leaped.

As soon as I felt that bar in my hands, I knew I'd made it. And I wasn't letting go.

"Sweet!" shouted Emilia.

When I dropped back down to the mat, McKenna was there with a high five and a hug. Even Avery said I was looking really strong. I flexed my biceps and laughed.

As I got back in line with my teammates, I stood a little taller.

With Avery's help, *maybe* I could do a cartwheel on the high beam. And if I could do a cartwheel on the high beam, maybe I could get my roundoff back handspring too.

But could I do it in just one week?

The Mock Meet
Chapter 5

The afternoon of the meet, Katie and I were twinning. We wore matching braids sprayed with glitter hair spray and our brand-new sparkly competition leos. But as soon as we got to Aberg's, Katie looked like she was going to be sick. Her face was pasty white, and she had a serious case of the hiccups.

"Are you okay?" Emilia asked, her eyes wide.

Katie shrugged.

"She's just nervous," I spoke for her. But I'd never seen Katie so quiet, or so pale.

"Me too!" said Emilia. "My hands are so sweaty, I'm afraid I'm going to peel right off the bars." She shook her hands and then her whole body in a kind of skeleton dance.

Emilia gets super talkative when she's nervous—the opposite of Katie. I was afraid chatty Emilia might be too much for Katie right now, so I steered her toward the tumbling line. "Let's warm up," I said.

Katie responded with a painful-sounding hiccup.

As we passed the chairs where our parents were sitting, Mom gave me a thumbs-up and Dad waggled his eyebrows. I laughed at my two biggest fans. If I did my best, I'd make them proud—*and* make the Gold team! A trickle of excitement ran down my spine.

Jack waved from the top of some stacked mats. "Hey, Katie!" he called. "Knock, knock."

"Jack, she doesn't have time—" I started to say.

But Katie was already answering. "Who's there?"

"Cows go."

"Cows go who?"

"No, silly," said Jack. "Cows go *moo.*"

"All right, all right," I said, tugging Katie toward the warm-up area. "We've got to *moove* on now."

When Katie laughed, her face finally relaxed. Maybe Jack was on to something with the jokes.

McKenna had us warm up, and then we split into two groups. Katie was starting on beam, and I was starting on floor. I gave her a quick hug for good luck.

I sat cross-legged beside the mats and watched Avery start her floor routine. She seemed so strong and confident, as usual. She didn't miss a beat.

When Emilia stood up to go next, I knew she was nervous, but it didn't show. She'd picked the perfect music for her routine—a song from a musical that started with a few dramatic notes. I saw her face change at the start of the song, like she was stepping onstage and knew exactly what character she was about to play.

Out of the corner of my eye, I saw Katie wobble on the beam and fall off. I wished I could do something to help my friend, but suddenly McKenna was nudging me. "Your turn," she whispered. "Remember to salute the judges!" She gave me a high five and a smile.

I must have floated onto the mats—I don't even remember walking. I saluted the judges, lifting my chin and chest and raising my arms overhead.

Then my music started, and my body knew just what to do. I'd practiced the routine a hundred times at the gym, in my living room, and in the backyard. But something felt different today. I felt stronger somehow. My dance moves were super snappy, and I was smiling so hard that my cheeks hurt.

When it was time for my tumbling pass, though, I still needed McKenna's spot. She met me on the mat, and as I launched into my back handspring, she helped me snap my legs and feet overhead and back down.

Keep going, I told myself. *Don't think about the spot.*

I soared through the rest of my routine, and then I sprinted off the mats. "Salute the judges!" McKenna reminded me. *Oops!* I ran back and gave a quick salute, heat rising to my cheeks.

McKenna stood by me while we waited for the judges

to hold up my score. When they did, McKenna squeezed my shoulder. I'd gotten an 8.475.

Is that good enough for Gold? I wondered as I followed my teammates toward the beam.

When it was my turn, my whole body flooded with ner-cited energy. My handstand felt tighter and stronger than ever, which gave me confidence going into my cartwheel. When I landed it, I heard cheering from somewhere nearby. I kept going, straight into my split leap. I don't think I've ever gotten so much height off the beam!

Something exploded in my chest—relief and excitement all rolled into one. I went into my dismount with so much energy that I couldn't stick my landing. I hopped backward instead. *Oops!* But I'd nailed my cartwheel on the high beam for the first time ever.

That joy took me through my bar routine and through vault. I had so much speed going on vault that I couldn't stick those landings either. But I was still smiling wide.

And then, before I knew it, it was time for awards.

McKenna invited us to sit on the floor while volunteers arranged mats to form a makeshift podium.

I spotted Katie's dark braids and rushed to her side. "That was *so* fun!" I said as I sat down beside her.

Katie finally had some color in her cheeks again. "I'm just glad it's over," she said, blowing out a breath of relief.

Then McKenna took the microphone. "Medals are awarded to fifty percent of participants at meets," she explained. "Our teams here at Aberg's are fairly small, so we'll be awarding first and second place winners on Gold, and only first place winners on Silver. But every girl here is a winner and will receive a medal for participation."

She smiled at us and then cleared her throat. "So, let's start with the Gold team. In second place on vault, with a score of 8.9, Emilia R.!"

I cheered for Emilia as she jumped up and stepped onto the second tier of the podium. I cheered for Avery, too, as she climbed onto the top tier.

Then I had a sinking thought: *I'm not going to medal today.* There were only three of us competing on Gold, and Avery and Emilia had stronger skills. They had been on the team longer than I had.

"Gymnasts salute!" said McKenna.

Emilia and Avery saluted the crowd while their parents took pictures. Then they hopped back down, and McKenna read off the winners on beam. "In second place on beam, with a score of 9.125, Lila M.!"

Wait, what?

"That's you!" said Katie, nudging me.

I stepped onto the podium, my legs shaking. When Avery climbed onto the top tier, she leaned over and whispered, "You got your cartwheel. Great job."

That meant almost as much to me as the medal McKenna hung around my neck.

I got another medal for second place on bars. When McKenna gave each of us a participation medal, too, I had three medals jingling around my neck! The sound reminded me of the wind chimes hanging from the tree in the Minneapolis Sculpture Garden. It sounded like success.

But when McKenna started announcing the winners for Silver, Katie withered beside me. Grace outscored Katie in every single event. By the time Katie stood up to get her participation medal, Grace was sporting four medals around her neck.

Katie tried to smile for a photo, but her mouth was pressed into a tight line. She eyed the door to the gym, like a horse about to bolt.

When she sat back down beside me, my own neck felt heavy with medals. I held them tight so they wouldn't jingle and make Katie feel bad.

McKenna pulled us into a team huddle and handed out slips of paper with our scores for each event. I studied mine:

Name __Lila__ Level __Gold__ Meet __Mock__

Vault	Bars	Beam	Floor	AA All Around
8.725	9.000	9.125	8.475	35.325

Had I done well enough to make the Gold team? I crossed my fingers beneath the score sheet.

"Those are pretty good scores for your first meet," said Avery, reading over my shoulder.

"Thanks!" I said, savoring Avery's compliment.

I glanced up just in time to see Katie shoving her score sheet into her backpack. She tugged on her warm-up jacket and headed for the door.

I started after her, but McKenna called me back. "Lila," she said, squeezing my hand, "I've never seen you shine quite so bright."

I beamed, glad that McKenna had seen on the outside what I'd felt on the inside. "I was really nervous," I admitted, "but I think I actually do *better* when I'm nervous!"

McKenna nodded. "Some gymnasts do. That adrenaline can make you a little faster and a little stronger. So, it's official now." McKenna held out her hand to shake mine. "Welcome to Xcel Gold," she said with a grin.

"Yes!" cried Emilia, pulling me into a side hug. "Congrats, teammate!"

Avery gave me a rare smile that told me she was happy to call me "teammate" too.

Then I felt Mom's hand on my shoulder. "Did I just hear what I think I heard?" she asked.

I nodded, smiling so wide I could barely speak.

I had earned my spot on Gold. I'd done my best in front of the judges, my coach, and my family. I'd rocked the mock meet. And I couldn't wait for more!

I found Katie in her room, hanging upside down over the side of her bed. She was wearing pajamas, her sparkly competition leo balled up on the floor. Harry was swatting at a strand of hair dangling from one of her braids.

When Katie saw me, she sighed. "That," she groaned, "was *not* fun."

I sank down on the floor beside her. "What happened?" I asked gently.

Katie shrugged. "Well, I didn't throw up, so that's good. But I went to the next level of nervousness. I couldn't remember my routines. My body wasn't working—I fell off the beam *twice*. And I totally biffed it on vault. Did you see me?"

I shook my head, feeling guilty that I hadn't even looked for Katie after I'd started my own events.

"Thank goodness we get to do vault twice," she said. "I wish I could have done every event twice—not that it would have mattered. I just would have been twice as nervous!"

I let Katie talk while I stroked Harry's back. When he rolled over and gave me his belly, I pulled my hand away. I know better than to pet Harry's stomach. I did it once, and he attacked my hand. But I *didn't* know what to say to my best friend.

"*You* did well though," she finally said. "Right?"

I shrugged. "I forgot to salute the judges, and I couldn't stick a single landing. But I did all right. I think I do better when I'm nervous. McKenna told me some gymnasts do."

Katie blew out her breath. "I'm definitely *not* one of those gymnasts. I fell to pieces in front of all those people— and those judges." She shuddered at the memory. Then her eyes brightened. "Wait, so did you make Gold?"

My face broke into a smile.

"Yes!" cried Katie, smacking my hand with a high five. "I'm glad one of us had a good day."

"Only because McKenna is such a great coach," I added. "She gave me extra time to get my skills this fall, and she gave me a spot on my back handspring today."

"She's the best," said Katie. Her eyes fell to her hands. "I hope I didn't disappoint her."

"It was just a practice meet," I reminded Katie. "And you won't have to worry about real meets for like another month. We can just focus on having fun, like going to

Honeycrisp Hill for Fall Fest next Saturday!"

Katie gave me a half smile.

"And Halloween is coming up," I reminded her. "We need to start thinking about costumes."

Katie sat upright. "Matching costumes?"

"Of course," I said. "We always wear matching costumes. It's tradition."

Katie is all about traditions, old ones and new ones. And making new traditions is easy, because we usually like all the same things.

Until now, I realized. I'd found out today that I love competing in front of judges and a crowd of people.

But Katie absolutely, one hundred percent does not.

McKenna's Secret
Chapter 6

So what did you all learn from the mock meet?" McKenna asked at the end of Tuesday night's practice.

I chewed on my lip, thinking. "That getting a spot on a skill is a big deduction," I said.

"So is falling," said Grace. She grimaced.

Avery nodded. "So is not sticking your landing, not pointing your toes . . ." She started ticking off deductions on her fingers.

I'd never really paid attention to scores before, but now that I'd competed in my first meet, I saw how much deductions mattered. "There's so much to remember!" I said.

McKenna gave me a reassuring smile. "We have a whole season to figure it out," she said. "We're only just getting started. What else did you girls learn?"

"That meets are *really* intense," said Katie, blowing out her cheeks.

Emilia laughed. "Right?" she said. "I've never been so nervous!"

"That's normal," McKenna said. "But it'll get easier. We'll work on ways for you to feel less nervous."

I suddenly remembered how calm Avery had seemed at the meet, just like she is at practice. "Avery didn't seem nervous," I pointed out.

Avery looked up in surprise. "I just try to focus on the skills," she said. "I tune out everything else."

"Yeah, I can't do that," said Emilia, shaking her head.

"Me neither," said Katie.

McKenna shrugged. "Every gymnast is different," she said. "But it sounds like you all learned something about yourselves that we can use to make the *next* meet better. We've got this." She caught Katie's eye and winked, which made my friend smile. "Go, Team Aberg?"

"Go, Team Aberg!" we all chimed in, slapping our hands on top of McKenna's.

As we left practice, I waved goodbye to Katie, whose mom had just pulled into the parking lot. Then I realized I'd forgotten my water bottle.

When I pushed back through the door of Aberg's, McKenna and Sawyer were chatting in the office. I went straight into the gym, grabbed my water bottle off the bench, and walked back through the lobby. When I stopped to tie my shoe, I overheard McKenna talking. "It's just hard being this far away from Seattle right now," she was saying. "I really miss my family."

Sawyer murmured something I couldn't understand. Then McKenna said, "I've been thinking about taking a break from school and coaching. I might head home for a while."

My stomach twisted. *A break? From coaching?*

"Please don't tell anyone," McKenna said to Sawyer. "Not until I decide."

When I heard Sawyer say goodbye, I panicked—she would walk out the door any second now and bust me for eavesdropping. So I stayed low, ducking below the window of the office and all the way out the front door.

"How was practice tonight?" Dad asked as I slid into the back seat.

"Good," I said. And that was the only thing I said all the way home.

I wanted to tell Dad what I'd heard, but McKenna didn't want anyone to know. I didn't want to spill her secret. But what if she actually went back to Seattle?

I couldn't even think about going to Aberg's without McKenna there. I'd only made the Xcel Gold team because she helped me so much! And we were just getting started— McKenna had said so herself. How could she think about leaving?

I swallowed the lump in my throat.

By the time we got home, I knew I had to find a way to get McKenna to stay in Minnesota. Even though she didn't want anyone to know she was thinking about leaving,

I had to tell Katie. I couldn't figure out a problem this big without her.

Instead of biking home after school on Wednesday, Katie and I biked straight to the park. It was our favorite thinking spot.

"I can't believe McKenna might leave," Katie groaned as we parked our bikes in the rack. "I've been thinking about it all day, ever since you told me. She's the best coach I've ever had—it's so unfair!"

"I know," I said. I scampered up the rope pyramid to the top and then moved my foot so Katie could sit below me. "She's homesick," I said. "I would be too if my family were that far away! She probably misses her little sisters."

Katie perked up at that. "Maybe *we* could be like her sisters. If she hangs out with us more, maybe she'll miss them less. What else do you know about her family?"

I thought again. "She used to have a goldendoodle named Cooper."

"Those are such cute dogs!" said Katie.

"Oh, and she likes horses!" I suddenly remembered. "She told me she used to volunteer at a horseback riding center when she was younger."

Katie's eyes lit up. "Ooh, maybe she can come to Honeycrisp Hill for Fall Fest on Saturday!"

Inviting McKenna to Honeycrisp Hill was the *perfect* idea. McKenna could meet Hollyhock! Maybe my favorite horse would work her magic, and McKenna would fall in love with her just like I had. "Katie," I said, "you're a genius."

She waved her hand dismissively. "Why do you sound so surprised?"

I would have laughed, but I was too busy figuring out how to get McKenna to Honeycrisp Hill. "Maybe Mom can email Mr. Benson and ask about McKenna coming. I'll ask Mom right away. C'mon!"

I flew down the rope structure so fast that I nearly fell. But there was no time to waste. Fall Fest was only three days away. Would Mr. Benson say yes? Would McKenna say yes?

I crossed my fingers and toes, hoping they would.

"Is McKenna here yet?" I craned my neck to look out the car window. We were pulling in to Honeycrisp Hill for Fall Fest, and McKenna had agreed to meet us here.

"Hey, you're squishing me!" Jack complained from his seat by the door.

Autumn had exploded at Honeycrisp Hill. The trees were crowned with red, orange, and yellow leaves. The Bensons had tied cornstalks around fence posts and placed pumpkins and gourds on bales of hay. Mighty Mae was racing around greeting everyone as if Fall Fest was her very own party.

Someone squealed as we got out of the car. When we turned around, Emilia pulled us into a group hug. Other campers were milling around the dining hall. When Jack spotted his favorite counselor, Luke, he bounded toward him like an eager puppy.

That's how I felt when I said hello to Hollyhock. Freya let me lead the horse into the grooming stall, and pretty soon Katie, Emilia, and I were brushing Hollyhock's golden coat.

"Don't stand too close," Freya reminded me, looking down at my feet. "We don't need another bruised toe."

I stepped back. I didn't want another injury, but I needed to be close to Hollyhock. When she leaned into me, giving one of her horse hugs, I leaned right back.

While Katie and Emilia brushed Hollyhock's neck and shoulders, I brushed her back and rump. "You get the front half, I'll get the back half," I said, knowing that Katie was afraid of getting kicked.

"Ooh," said Katie. "That gives me an idea for our Halloween costume. We could be a palomino horse, like Hollyhock. One of us could be her front half and the other could be her back half!"

"I love that idea!" I said. "Katie, you're—"

"A genius," she said, finishing my sentence. "I know."

As I wove Hollyhock's tail into a fishtail braid, someone called softly, "Do you have room for one more in there?"

I spun around and saw McKenna. "You're here!" I whisper-shouted, not wanting to spook Hollyhock.

"I am," said McKenna as Freya opened the stall gate. "And this must be Hollyhock. She's absolutely beautiful."

I felt a rush of pride. Hollyhock isn't my horse, but sometimes it feels like she is.

McKenna spoke gently to Hollyhock and approached her from the side, so Hollyhock would see her coming. Then she reached out to stroke her shoulder.

"You know your way around horses," said Freya with a look of approval.

"I used to volunteer at a riding center in Seattle," McKenna said. "I've missed being around horses."

When Freya offered her a brush to use on Hollyhock, McKenna took it. "Nice fishtail braid," she said, admiring Hollyhock's tail. "My little sisters and I used to wear our hair like that."

Katie shot me a look. "Your sisters?" she asked.

McKenna nodded. "Mara and Maisey. They're twins but we'd sometimes all wear our hair the same way."

"We should all do our hair the same right now," Katie said eagerly. "Then *we* could look like sisters!"

I saw where Katie was going with this. "I'll do the braiding," I said. "There are plenty of hair ties."

Katie wrinkled her nose. "Don't use that horse comb on me, though."

I laughed and washed my hands. Then I got started on Katie's braids. I had done her hair hundreds of times, and I'd even done Emilia's hair for the riding demo at camp. But I hadn't done McKenna's hair since I was little and she was my babysitter.

McKenna's hair is long and caramel colored, like mine. It's thicker, though, and smells like flowers. It took me a while to get her braid just right. Hollyhock kept nosing at my arm as if to say, *Don't forget about me here!*

When I was done, Freya took a picture of us. "Oh, we do look like sisters!" said McKenna as she zoomed in on the photo.

Katie and I locked eyes. I could tell she was thinking the same thing I was: Were we helping McKenna feel less homesick?

Baby Goats

Chapter 7

When Freya said it was time to visit the goats, Katie made a beeline for the stall door. I wasn't ready to leave Hollyhock, though. I wrapped my arms around her neck and gave her one last hug.

"You can ride her in a little bit," Freya promised. "But first, let's go see those goats. I have a surprise for you."

When we got to the goat pen, two of the goats were inside the pen and one was out. "Nibbles!" I cried. He was the goat that had roamed freely during the summer.

Nibbles bleated. When he started nibbling on Katie's shoelaces, she laughed and tried to tug her foot away.

"That's why he's called Nibbles," Emilia explained. "You'll get used to him!"

McKenna reached over the fence to pet the other goats, who got up on their hind legs to greet her. Then she gestured toward another pen with high plywood walls. "Are there more goats in there?"

Freya's eyes twinkled. "Go take a look," she said.

Katie reached the pen first. "Baby goats!" she squealed.

"Gretta had her kids!" Freya announced. "They're about four weeks old. Aren't they cute? Pepper is the black and white one, and Olive is light brown."

Katie leaned so far into the pen, I was afraid she'd fall in. "They're so playful!" she said as the goats romped around their mother. "Ooh, good jump, Olive!"

The little brown goat could jump so high, she looked like she was launching off a trampoline rather than the straw-covered ground. When I laughed, she scampered toward me, making tiny, high-pitched bleating sounds.

"Cuteness overload," said Emilia, leaning over the pen. "I can't take it!"

"Cutest twins ever," I agreed, reaching down to scratch Pepper's neck. His fur was super soft.

"Twins?" Katie repeated. "Just like McKenna's sisters!"

"Actually," said Freya, "they're triplets. But Buttons, the smallest kid, wasn't getting enough milk and had to be separated. Mrs. Benson keeps her in a pen in the kitchen and is bottle-feeding her until she gets stronger."

"Aw," said Katie. "Poor thing! She must be so lonely, being so far away from her family. I would hate that."

"Me too," said McKenna sadly.

I shot Katie a look. McKenna *was* far away from her family. We'd invited her here to make her feel less homesick, not more homesick!

When Katie realized what she'd said, she grimaced. "Can we meet Buttons?" she asked Freya. "I'd love to see Mrs. Benson feeding her. I bet that's adorable."

Freya pulled out her phone. "Let me text Mrs. Benson and ask her."

Katie crossed her fingers until Freya's phone dinged. "Yes!" said Freya, smiling. "Looks like we can do a quick visit with Buttons before riding this afternoon."

We headed down to the farmhouse, where Mrs. Benson met us on the porch. She wore her silver hair in a low pony-tail and had a kind smile. I liked her instantly.

"C'mon in," she said, waving us into the kitchen.

McKenna crossed the room toward the woodstove and held out her hands to feel the heat. "It's so toasty in here!" she said.

"We keep the stove going for Buttons," Mrs. Benson explained. "Goats are usually born in the spring, so when they're born this late in the year and are underweight, like Buttons, we want to keep them warm." She gestured to a pen right there in the kitchen "Ready to meet our newest addition?"

I craned my neck to see. In the corner of the pen, a tiny goat nosed at the straw. She was smaller than Pepper and Olive and all white, except for a little smudge of brown.

"That's Buttons," said Mrs. Benson. "Isn't she cute as a button?"

At the sound of Mrs. Benson's voice, Buttons scampered over to us.

"Aw," said Katie, dropping to her knees by the pen. "Is she hungry?"

"Always," said Mrs. Benson. "Would you like to feed her?"

Katie gasped. "Can we?" she asked. "How?"

Mrs. Benson handed her a bottle. "You can go in the pen. Buttons knows what to do."

Katie waved me into the pen with her. When she sat down, Buttons climbed right into her lap. "I'll hold her and you hold the bottle," said Katie.

Buttons went right for the nipple and started guzzling the milk, her little tail wagging excitedly.

"Look at her tail!" Emilia exclaimed.

Mrs. Benson laughed "She wags it when she's excited. And nothing makes her more excited than a fresh bottle of milk."

Katie grinned at me. Nothing made *Katie* more excited than spending time with baby animals. If she could sprout a tail, it would be wagging like crazy right now.

"She's drinking so fast," said McKenna. "Slow down, sweetie!"

Buttons drank until her white belly was round and full. Then she nosed at my fingers, licking them to make sure she got every droplet of milk. It tickled in the sweetest way.

We all gave Buttons little pets on her neck and back. Then Freya checked her phone and said it was time to do some riding.

My stomach fluttered with excitement. I hadn't ridden Hollyhock since the end of summer! But Katie's face fell. She was going to have a hard time leaving Buttons, just like I'd had a hard time leaving Hollyhock in the barn.

"You get to learn how to ride a horse today," I reminded Katie as I led her out of the kitchen. But I don't think she heard me. Katie looked back at Buttons until the screen door swung shut. Then she looked at me with wide eyes. "I'm ner-cited," she said, using my family's code word. "A little more 'ner' than 'cited'."

I tugged at her braid. "You'll do great!" As we headed up the hill to the barn, I caught up with McKenna. "Are you going to ride?" I asked, hoping she'd say yes.

McKenna nodded. "Mr. Benson invited me to ride because I have some experience. It's been a while, though!"

"It'll all come back," said Emilia. "It's like riding a bike."

"Riding Hollyhock is *nothing* like riding a bike," I countered. "It's way better!"

Freya laughed. "I agree." Then she turned to Katie. "Have you ridden before?"

Katie hesitated. "Sort of," she said.

I whirled around to face her. "Really?" I said. "I didn't know that. When?"

"At the Como Park Zoo," said Katie with a grin. "Remember?"

I thought back to the last time we'd been to the zoo in

Saint Paul. We had walked through the botanical gardens, hung out in the Como Town amusement park, and ridden horses on the old carousel. "Katie," I said, playfully slapping her shoulder. "Those were fake horses."

She shrugged. "But you ride them the same. Climb on and hang on tight, right?"

Freya laughed. "It's not *quite* the same thing," she said, "but I like your confidence. We'll start in the indoor arena, just to be safe."

As soon as we started riding, Katie looked anything but confident. She was on Ben, the slowest and gentlest horse in the herd. He was twenty-two years old, which Mr. Benson had told us was like sixty-five in human years.

Freya walked beside Katie, giving her pointers about how to hold the reins and squeeze her legs to get Ben going faster. But when Freya let Katie try riding on her own, Ben stopped.

"Relax the reins," said Freya. "If you hold them too tight, Ben thinks you want him to stop."

Katie sighed. "I'm confusing him. I'm sorry, Ben. I really don't speak horse."

I felt bad for Katie, but it felt so *good* to ride Hollyhock again. The afternoon sun streamed through the rafters, and birds chirped overhead. Hollyhock pranced around the sawdust floor, her head held high.

Katie didn't know how to speak horse, but I did. I just

had to *look* where I wanted to go, and Hollyhock felt my body shift and turned in that direction. With the gentlest squeeze of my legs, she picked up the pace. Soon, we were trotting, the leather saddle squeaking beneath my seat.

"Good girl," I said. As Hollyhock settled back into a smooth walk, I reached down to pat her neck.

McKenna rode in front of us on Cinnamon, a sassy chestnut mare. As McKenna trotted around the arena, she smiled, her cheeks pink. She looked so happy!

Behind me, Katie had completely given up. She wasn't even holding the reins anymore. While Freya led Ben, Katie gripped the saddle horn as if she were holding the pole of a horse on a carousel ride.

I had thought Katie would love riding horses as much as I do. Nobody loves animals more than Katie! And we usually like all the same things.

But Katie clearly didn't love riding. She looked as uneasy on horseback as she had at the meet. When Freya said our time in the ring was almost up, I could see the relief wash across Katie's face.

Then Mr. Benson stepped into the arena and waved at me. "How's our girl doing today?" he asked.

I knew he meant Hollyhock. Mr. Benson and I had worked together to help Hollyhock overcome her fear of dogs, so she kind of *was* our girl. "She's amazing," I said, leaning over to hug Hollyhock's neck.

Then Mr. Benson turned to McKenna. "Is Cinnamon behaving herself?" he asked.

McKenna nodded. "We're good friends already," she said, giving Cinnamon a pat.

"Well, I hope you'll come back again," said Mr. Benson. "Horse lovers are always welcome here, especially during the offseason. We need to give our horses all the exercise they can get."

"Can we come back, too?" Katie asked.

I was surprised to hear her chime in. She was still hanging on to the saddle horn for dear life.

"To check on Buttons," Katie clarified.

I laughed. Katie was smitten with that baby goat.

By the time we left Honeycrisp Hill, we had made plans to come back next weekend. I'd get to see Hollyhock again. Katie could visit Buttons. And hopefully McKenna would feel less homesick, and decide to never ever leave Minnesota.

That was my plan, anyway.

Ready to Ride

Chapter 8

L et's try it one more time," said McKenna.

It was Tuesday night at practice, and she stood beside me on the mat, ready to spot my back handspring. *Again.*

I squatted low, like I was about to sit in a chair.

"Watch your knees," said McKenna. "Make sure they're directly over your feet or you won't get enough umph out of your jump."

"Right," I said, pulling my knees back. Then, on McKenna's cue, I pushed up through my toes and swung my arms overhead.

"Follow your hands with your eyes," McKenna reminded me.

I arched my back and reached for the floor behind me. But when I tried to snap my legs over my head, I felt McKenna's hands helping me over.

"Okay, pop back up," McKenna reminded me when I landed.

My pop felt more like a fizzle. I blew out a breath of

frustration. "Why is it still so hard? I almost did it at the mock meet!"

McKenna smiled. "You got an extra burst of adrenaline that day," she said. "But on a normal day, you have to rely on strength and form. Let's do some handstand snap-down drills to help with the skill."

McKenna pulled over a stacked panel mat and demonstrated the drill. She leaned forward into a handstand on the stacked mat. "Open your armpits and keep your arms by your ears," she said.

McKenna's handstand was strong and steady. "Then push off through your shoulders and snap your feet back down." McKenna snapped out of her handstand, landing on the floor. "Want to try it?"

I nodded. "I'll try anything," I mumbled. I tried to mimic what McKenna had done. My handstand was wobbly, but I pushed off through my shoulders and snapped my feet back down.

"Good!" she said. "Just like that. If you do ten of those every day," said McKenna, "you'll have that back handspring in no time."

She looked at me so intently that I believed her—every word. If McKenna thought I could do it, I *knew* I could! And I had three and a half weeks before our next meet. Doing the math in my head, that meant 240 snap-downs. Now I had a goal to work on.

I went into my next handstand feeling strong, but as soon as I felt McKenna's hands supporting me, I couldn't help but think, *What if McKenna leaves?*

When we moved to beam, Katie was already sharing a beam with Grace, so I joined Avery. She was doing one of her perfect handstands, strong and steady just like McKenna's.

"You're so good at that!" I said as she stood back up. "I wish I could do handstands like yours."

Avery hopped off the beam and fixed her ponytail. "I can help you," she said. "Here, show me yours."

I showed off my best handstand, but my legs were wobbly and not nearly as straight as Avery's had been.

She had feedback for me right away. "Try spider fingers," she said. "Spread your fingers more so you can really wrap them around the beam."

"Okay," I said, giving it another go. The tip helped. I did feel stronger and steadier.

"Keep your legs together," Avery called from the mat. "Point your toes—it's a deduction if you don't."

"Thanks!" I said brightly. "I'm going to work on spider fingers for now."

Avery shrugged and then turned to watch Katie and Grace. Katie was doing split jumps. She could get as much air as I could on my jumps, but she wasn't quite as flexible.

"Your legs weren't at ninety degrees, Katie," said Avery. "You need more split."

Katie wobbled and jumped off the beam. "Huh?" she said.

"You need to work on your flexibility," said Avery.

Katie furrowed her brow. "Thanks," she said. "I'll do that."

Katie left the high beam and strode straight to the low beam, which was as far away from Avery as she could get. I could almost see the steam coming out of Katie's ears.

I hopped off my beam and followed her. "Don't worry about Avery," I whispered. "She's got four younger siblings at home, so she's used to telling people what to do."

Katie's eyes flashed. "Well I'm not her little sister," she said. "When she watches me, I get nervous and then I mess up even more."

"I know she can be intense," I said. "But she's just trying to help the team."

I felt a hand on my shoulder. "Everything all right, girls?" asked McKenna.

Katie rolled her eyes with exasperation. "I'm getting advice from Avery," she said.

"I see," McKenna said. "Avery is just trying to—"

"Help the team," Katie finished. "I know, I know."

McKenna smiled gently. "I'll remind Avery that you already have a coach."

Katie blew out a breath of relief. "Thanks," she said.

Once again, McKenna had made everything better. *Best coach ever,* said the voice in my head. *She can't leave!*

"That's my song," cried Katie. "Turn it up!"

It was Saturday afternoon—after my gymnastics practice and Katie's dance lesson—and McKenna was driving us back to Honeycrisp Hill. Katie's floor routine music had just come on the radio, and Katie was belting out every word.

"Sing it, Lila!" Katie handed me a fake microphone, a rolled-up magazine she'd found tucked behind the seat.

I grabbed it and waited to sing the only words I knew— the chorus. "Throw away your fear and take a chance. All we gotta do is dance, dance, dance!"

McKenna bobbed her head and shoulders, dancing along. She caught my eye in the mirror and grinned.

Katie and I hadn't been in McKenna's little blue Honda since we were seven. She'd take us to the park or the movies sometimes when she babysat. The car looked just how I remembered it, only now there was a silver star pendant dangling from the rearview mirror.

"Is that necklace new?" I asked McKenna, pointing.

She shook her head. "My grandma gave that to me when I was your age," she said. "She gave matching necklaces to my sisters. 'Stars for my stars,' she said. It was her way of reminding us that she'd always be cheering us on."

"What are your sisters like?" Katie asked.

McKenna smiled. "Mara and Maisey have totally different personalities. They look alike, with brown eyes and wavy brown hair. But Maisey can't sit still—she has to be moving all the time. And Mara? She could sit for hours reading or working on her art."

When McKenna fell silent, Katie and I looked at each other. Had we said something wrong?

"I'll bet you miss your sisters," I finally said. "But if it helps, Katie and I could be like your little sisters in Minnesota."

McKenna glanced over her shoulder and gave me a warm smile. "Thanks, Lila," she said. "Spending time with you two definitely helps."

Katie's knee started bouncing with happiness. We laughed and sang the rest of the way to Honeycrisp Hill. As we pulled into the gravel driveway that led to the farmhouse, Katie called out the window. "We're coming, Buttons. We're coming!"

"You're obsessed," I joked as we got out of the car.

But as soon as we saw sweet Buttons, I got it—the tiny white goat was just as excited to see us as we were to see her. Her little tail wagged and she jumped up and down, trying to get out of the pen.

"You've gotten so big!" Katie crooned as she squatted beside the pen.

Katie looked to Mrs. Benson with pleading eyes. "Can I feed her?"

"Not yet! It's time for our ride," I reminded Katie. "You can feed her after."

Katie's shoulders slumped. "I'm feeling more like baby goats than big horses today." She looked at me apologetically.

"Okaaay," I said, feeling kind of hurt. Riding Hollyhock was my favorite thing in the world. But Katie didn't care about riding at all. She'd much rather feed a baby goat than get back in the saddle with Ben.

"You're welcome to stay here with me and Buttons," said Mrs. Benson. "You're good with her, and Buttons is going a little stir-crazy with no one to play with."

"Oh, I'll play with you, Buttons," said Katie. "I know you miss your sister and brother."

So McKenna and I left Katie in the kitchen while we traipsed up the hill to the barn. I could feel McKenna's eyes on me as we walked.

"Are you disappointed Katie's not riding today?" she asked.

I shrugged. "I just don't understand why she doesn't love horses," I confessed. "We usually like all the same things."

McKenna smiled. "No two people like *all* the same things," she said. "Not even my twin sisters, remember?"

I nodded, but I didn't really agree with her. Katie and

I had *always* liked all the same things, ever since we were little. Wasn't that part of being best friends?

When we reached the barn, Freya was in a stall, putting a saddle on Cinnamon. "You're here!" she said. "Where's Katie?"

"She's going to hang with Buttons," I said, trying to hide the disappointment in my voice.

"I can't blame her," said Freya. "Buttons is adorable." She tightened the strap on Cinnamon's saddle. "You and McKenna are both experienced riders, so how about taking a little trail ride this afternoon?"

I nodded eagerly, but butterflies filled my stomach. "I haven't gone on a trail ride with Hollyhock since last summer," I reminded Freya, "when she spooked at a dog and ..."

"And you fell off?" said Freya. "I remember that day. It was scary. But you and Hollyhock have both come a long way since then."

I nodded and stood a little taller. "Is Hollyhock all saddled up?" I asked.

In response, a stall door shook. When I rushed down the aisle to greet her, Hollyhock nosed at the door as if she couldn't wait to get out.

"She's been cooped up in there all day," Freya explained. "Her buddy Dakota has an abscess—a sore hoof. She needs to stay in the stall to keep her hoof clean, and having

Hollyhock in the next stall calms her down."

I stepped sideways until I could see the paint horse in the neighboring stall. She was eating hay, her dark mane falling across her white forehead. "I'm sorry about your abscess, Dakota," I said. "I know what a sore foot feels like."

McKenna chuckled as she stepped into the barn. "Yes, you do," she said.

"And hanging out with my buddy helped me too," I said, remembering Purple Tuesday with Katie at the gym. I wished Katie were in the barn with us right now. But what could I do? I couldn't *make* her love horses.

"Hello, Hollyhock," McKenna called over my shoulder. "You're ready to ride, aren't you?"

Hollyhock answered with a whinny. She pawed at the ground with her hoof.

"She's ready," said Freya with a laugh. "Do you two want to saddle her up while I go get Ben?"

"Yes!" I said. I jogged to the tack room and found Hollyhock's special pink saddle.

Soon, we were following Freya and Cinnamon past the paddocks and out toward the riding trails. McKenna was behind me on Ben, clucking her tongue to urge him along. She knew how to coax him to do better, just like she did with us at the gym.

Hollyhock was alert and full of energy as we passed

through the trail gate. Her ears pricked forward, listening to the sounds of the woods. Sunlight filtered through the trees, casting shadows on the trail. Leaves drifted gently downward.

"You're doing great, Hollyhock," I said, patting her neck. "You're safe out here."

"You have a very reassuring voice," McKenna called. "I'm sure that helps Hollyhock feel steady."

"Mr. Benson taught me that," I said. Then I turned to smile at McKenna. "Isn't it great out here?"

"Beautiful," said McKenna.

Ben nickered, as if in agreement.

When Freya and Cinnamon led us down a slope, I leaned back in my saddle for balance. I pulled on the reins just a little so that Hollyhock wouldn't get too close to Cinnamon. If she did, Cinnamon might kick to tell her to back off.

As we rode farther, I realized we'd reached the part of the trail where I had fallen last summer. I could play back every detail in my mind: The squirrel scampering out of the bush. The dog bursting across the trail behind it. And Hollyhock snorting and stepping sideways.

When I pulled Hollyhock to a stop, McKenna and Ben rode up next to us. "This is where I fell," I told McKenna.

She nodded and glanced around at the trail. "I've fallen too. It's scary, I know. But it's good that you can ride here again and not be nervous."

I took a deep breath and realized that I *wasn't* nervous. I stroked Hollyhock's neck and told her what a good girl she was. And just like that, the memory passed.

Freya pulled back on Cinnamon's reins up ahead. "Which way, girls?" We had come to a fork in the trail.

"That path goes deeper into the woods," Freya explained, pointing right. "And the other one runs closer to the farm fence line."

McKenna shrugged and laughed. "I have a tough time making decisions," she said. "You choose."

I pointed right, not wanting our trail ride to end too soon. But as I nudged Hollyhock onward, I thought about McKenna's words: *I have a tough time making decisions.* Did that mean she was struggling to decide whether to stay in Saint Paul or go home to Seattle?

I wish she'd let me make that decision for her too, I thought sadly. I would choose to keep McKenna here forever and never let her go.

"Did you have fun on the trail?" asked Mr. Benson when we got back to the farmhouse. He was sitting on the porch swing with a cup of coffee.

"So much fun," McKenna answered. "It's wonderful to ride again, especially in such a beautiful place." She gazed back appreciatively at the rolling hills and green

pastures of Honeycrisp Hill.

Just then, Katie burst through the screen door with Buttons in her arms. The tiny goat bleated a hello. "Buttons is famous!" Katie said to me. "Mrs. Benson posts videos of her online and she's gotten hundreds of likes."

"Wow," I said, holding out my hand so that Buttons could nibble on my fingers. "Good for you, Buttons."

"So we can see how she's doing even when we can't visit," said Katie breathlessly. "Isn't that cool?"

"Very cool," I said. After riding Hollyhock with McKenna, I no longer felt hurt that Katie had stayed back with Buttons. How could I? My best friend was happy, McKenna was happy, and in that moment, I was happy, too.

Busted!

Chapter 9

When McKenna dropped Katie and me off at my house Saturday afternoon, Dad met us on the porch.

"So who's going to be the head and who's going to be the rump?" he asked, his eyes twinkling. He pulled something out from behind his back: a big green package with the words "Costume Express" printed on the side.

"Our Halloween costume!" Katie cried, jumping up and down.

I tore the package open and pulled out the velvety cream-colored horse costume. It came in four parts: The head, back, and rump were all one piece. There were two sets of horse legs, which Katie and I instantly pulled on over our pants. And there were hooves to cover our shoes.

"Help us with the head, Dad," I said.

He dropped the horse head over mine, adjusting it so that I could see through the eyeholes. Then he laid the back and rump of the horse over Katie.

I heard the squeak of the front door and then Jack's voice. "What are you supposed to be? A camel?"

"No, Jack," I groaned. "A horse—obviously."

"Then why is there a bump on the horse's back?"

"Oops," said Katie in a muffled voice. "That's my head. I guess I have to bend over."

She leaned forward and put her hands around my waist. "Should we try walking?"

"Careful on the steps!" said Dad.

"How about if we count?" I said. "Left, right, left, right—not so tight, Katie. You're pulling my horse pants down!"

"Sorry!" she said, laughing.

Together, *very* slowly, we walked down the steps and across the yard. Then I felt Katie duck out of the costume. "Whew, it's hot in there!" she said. "And it doesn't really look like Hollyhock."

I took the horse head off and examined it. "You're right. There's no white blaze, like Hollyhock's." I stared down at my horse legs. "No white stockings either."

"Can we fix that?" asked Katie. "Maybe with white paint?"

"Yes!" I said. "Katie, you're a—"

"I know, I know," she said, holding up her hand. "But thank you." She took a bow, nearly losing her horse pants in the process. "Should we paint them on now?"

I shook my head. "Let's practice gymnastics first."

Katie slid off her horse hooves. "But you had practice this morning!"

"I know," I said, "but I'm trying to get in extra practice every day. Our meet is only three weeks away!"

Katie sighed and plopped down in the grass, struggling with the palomino pants. "I can't even think about it yet," she said. "I'll freak out."

"I know. I'm sorry," I said. "But I want to get my back handspring down without a spot so that I can get a decent score—better than last time. And I want to make the podium again."

I regretted it as soon as I'd said it. Katie hadn't made the podium at all during the mock meet. The only medal she had earned was for participation.

She looked up at me with a weird expression, her head cocked to the side. "You're changing," she said. "You used to have fun with gymnastics, just like me. But now it seems like you're all about getting high scores and winning medals."

She didn't sound angry—more curious, as if she were doing a science experiment and had gotten a strange result.

"What do you mean?" I said. "I still have fun! I just want to keep getting better and better. Don't you?"

Katie picked up a dry leaf and crumbled it between her fingers. She shrugged. "I guess so," she said.

When a breeze blew through the yard, I shivered. "C'mon," I said. "Let's go ask my dad about some white paint before it gets dark."

As Katie and I hurried up the porch steps, the horse costume felt heavy in my hands. *Am I changing?* I wondered. *And if I am, is that so bad?*

Tuesday night at gymnastics, I was determined to get my back handspring. I'd been doing snap-down drills for a week. I could do my back handspring on the trampoline, so I knew how it was supposed to feel. And McKenna barely needed to help my legs over at all anymore.

When she stepped onto the mat to spot me, I shook my head. "Can I try it on my own?" I asked.

McKenna smiled. "Absolutely," she said. "But let's pull over the sting mat just to be safe."

Sawyer helped McKenna pull the thin black mat into position.

"All right, let's see it, Lila," said McKenna. "You've got this!"

I felt everyone's eyes on me as I squatted low in front of the mat. I took a deep breath. Then, with everything I had, I threw my arms overhead and launched backward. I drove my legs up as my hands touched the floor, and then snapped my legs back down—just like I'd done a hundred times during snap-down drills.

When I landed, I popped back up, jumping forward the way I'd been practicing. As I raised my arms overhead, happiness exploded in my chest. I'd done it! I'd actually done it!

"Beautiful!" McKenna cried, giving me a hug.

Sawyer gave me a high five. "Nice job!"

Katie and Emilia started pumping their fists in the air. "I'd give that a 9.9!" said Katie.

"A perfect 10!" said Emilia. "You should take a bow."

Avery's forehead wrinkled, like she was about to give me some deductions. But I was flying so high, I didn't care.

Instead of celebrating, I lined right up in front of the sting mat and did the back handspring again. And again. When I started breathing hard, McKenna said I should probably take a break, just to stay safe.

"Water break!" she called.

Katie met me at the water fountain with a fist bump. "I can't believe you got your back handspring!" she said, her eyes flashing.

"It was because of McKenna," I said, which was the truth. "It's those drills she showed me how to do at home."

"Best coach ever," said Katie with a sigh. "She *can't* go back to Seattle."

"What?" asked Avery.

We whirled around to see Avery standing right behind Katie. Emilia was there too, her mouth hanging open. "Wait, what?" she said. "Is McKenna leaving?"

Katie slapped her hand over her mouth, which pretty much answered Emilia's question.

"We don't know for sure," I whispered, trying to do damage control. "She *might* be leaving but she hasn't decided yet. Don't say anything to her, okay?"

But Avery was already crossing the mat toward McKenna. She tugged on McKenna's sleeve and whispered something in her ear. McKenna's eyebrows shot up, and she looked at me.

Busted! I thought, ducking my head low. I had tried to keep her secret, but I'd failed. Would she be mad?

Right away, McKenna called a team huddle. "I'm sorry you girls have been wondering and worrying about my future plans," she said, looking mostly at me and Katie. "The truth is, I *am* homesick for Seattle. My grandma has been having some health issues, and I'm worried about her."

"The grandma who gave you the star necklace?" I asked.

McKenna nodded solemnly. "We're really close," she said. "It's hard to be so far away from home right now."

My heart hurt for McKenna. I couldn't imagine being so far away from my family, especially if one of them were sick.

"I don't have plans to leave anytime soon," McKenna promised us, "so I want you to stay focused here at the gym. We've got a meet to prepare for!" She tried to sound bright and cheery, but sadness tugged at the corners of her mouth.

Then I noticed my teammates' faces. Emilia was nibbling vigorously on a fingernail. And Avery's normally composed face looked pink and blotchy. Katie looked as pale as she had on the day of the mock meet.

I felt bad for McKenna, but I felt bad for my teammates too. Because now they all looked just as worried as Katie and I had been feeling. Why did Katie have to spill McKenna's secret?

A Storm Brews

Chapter 10

When Katie and I got to my house after school on Wednesday, a light rain was falling. We pulled our bikes onto the porch and shook out our jackets.

"It's so gloomy!" said Katie. "Everything is yucky and mucky." She scraped her muddy shoes on the steps.

I think she meant the weather, but our moods had been pretty gloomy since gymnastics last night. Now that the whole team knew McKenna might leave, the possibility seemed more real.

"We need to bust out of this funk," I said.

Katie raised an eyebrow. "Goat cam?" she said, fishing her phone out of her pocket. That's what she called the Buttons videos Mrs. Benson posted every few days. "I want to see if Buttons has grown."

"Katie, we were at Honeycrisp Hill four days ago," I reminded her. "You just saw her!"

Katie shrugged. "She could have grown a little—she ate like a horse on Saturday. And she needs to grow if she's ever going to get back together with her siblings. Oh, look!"

Katie pulled up a video of Buttons chasing after Mr. Benson's foot. "She's so cute! Oh, there you go, Buttons. Get that shoe, girl."

We watched the video three times, and then Katie set her phone down. "Now what should we do?" she asked. "Any great ideas?"

"Gymnastics?" I said. "The yard is too wet, but we could work on my practice beam in the basement."

Katie groaned. "Gymnastics, gymnastics, gymnastics. We never just have fun anymore."

Katie's words felt like a slap. "Since when is gymnastics not fun?" I asked.

Katie flopped down into the porch swing. "I don't know. Since the mock meet, I guess."

I sighed. "I get that the meet was hard for you, Katie, but our real meet is only two and a half weeks away! I just did my first back handspring without a spot last night, and there's a lot more I need to practice before the meet."

Katie picked up her phone again, as if she didn't want to hear what I had to say. I tried again. "We've been sitting at school all day," I said, keeping my voice light. "Aren't you itching to move? I am!"

Katie only shrugged.

I felt like Hollyhock stuck in a stall next to her buddy with the sore hoof. I wanted to get out and run, but Katie couldn't—or *wouldn't*.

I swallowed my disappointment and came up with an idea I knew Katie would love. "We finished painting our horse costume," I said, "but we don't have any trick-or-treat bags. Want to make some?"

She perked right up. "Horse themed?" she said. "Like grain buckets or something?"

I nodded. "Big ones. To hold lots of candy—sweet for me and sour for you."

Before this fall, the only thing Katie and I had disagreed on was which candy was the best. I liked chocolate, but Katie liked sour fruit flavors.

Now it seemed like there were so many *other* things we disagreed on. *I can't believe gymnastics is one of them,* I thought as I followed Katie into the house.

I knew something was different as soon as I walked into the gym Thursday night. Katie was huddled around the water fountain with Grace and Emilia. Avery sat slumped on the bench, picking at the stickers on her water bottle. Everyone looked grim.

"Over here, girls," Sawyer called from the warm-up area.

I hurried over to the mat. "Where's McKenna?" I blurted.

Sawyer took a deep breath. "She got called home for a family emergency."

"Is it her grandma?" Katie asked as she sat down beside me.

Sawyer nodded. "She needs surgery."

"Oh, no," I whispered.

"Is she going to be okay?" asked Emilia. She shook her hands, as if trying to shake off the bad news.

"I don't know," said Sawyer. "I hope so."

"Are *we* going to be okay?" I asked, thinking out loud.

Sawyer straightened up. "Yes," she said. "We're going to be just fine. I'll be coaching you until McKenna gets back."

"When will that be?" Avery asked, a little too quickly.

Sawyer sighed. "I'm not sure," she said. "McKenna wants to be back in time to help you prep for your first meet, but if she can't be, I'll be there to help you."

"But you're an *assistant* coach," said Avery. I knew she wasn't trying to be mean. She was worried. Until this fall, Sawyer had only worked with little kids.

Sawyer's mouth tightened. "We'll get through this," she said. "Let's go ahead and get started with warm-ups." She stood up and brushed off her joggers.

"Wait," Grace piped up, "you're not doing it right."

"Excuse me?" said Sawyer, her voice rising.

"You have to say, 'Ready to work?'" Grace reminded her.

Uff. We were only thirty seconds into practice without McKenna, and already things were falling apart.

Sawyer flushed. "Sorry," she said. "Ready to work?"

"Ready to fly," we all murmured. But it sounded more like we were ready to take a nap, or crawl into a hole. How could we practice without our favorite coach? And what if we had to compete in two weeks without her?

During stretches, when Sawyer went to get a clipboard, Emilia launched into full-on worry mode. "What if McKenna doesn't come back in time for the meet?" she asked. "What if she never comes back—and we didn't even get to say goodbye?"

Grace leaned forward into a frog stretch, propping herself up on her elbows. "It'll be okay," she said. "Sawyer is a good coach. I had her last year when I was on Bronze."

"But she's an *assistant*," Avery said again. "I mean, she's nice, but she doesn't really know how to coach Silver and Gold—not yet."

Katie sank into the splits, wincing a little. "Maybe McKenna will come back in time," she said.

"Maybe," I echoed, wanting to believe it.

When we stood for warm-ups, Avery lifted her chin. "If she doesn't come back in time, we'll be all right," she said. "I've competed at plenty of meets. I can help get everyone ready."

A shadow fell across Katie's face. "Great," she whispered to me. "That's all we need—Avery being helpful."

Avery focused her attention on Grace during vault practice. Then we moved to floor. Katie was working on her roundoff backward roll. The moment she came up and out of the roll, Avery started to give advice.

Katie's eyes flashed. "Avery, stop being so critical!" Katie snapped.

"Huh?" said Avery, taking a step back.

"You're way too intense," said Katie. "Even Lila thinks so."

When Avery looked at me, I saw surprise in her eyes. My stomach lurched. "I don't think that—" I started to say.

"Yes you do!" Katie countered. "You just said it to me last week."

My mind raced back to that conversation. Maybe I had said those words, and they were kind of true. But I'd said them in private. Why did Katie have to repeat them to Avery?

"I only meant that Avery is really, um ... focused," I stammered.

Katie put her hand on her hip. "That is not what you meant." She stormed off, mad at me now too.

This time, I didn't go after her. How could Katie have called me out like that?

McKenna was gone and our team was falling apart. If McKenna didn't come back soon, our first meet was going to be a *total* disaster.

Taking Sides
Chapter 11

After gymnastics practice Saturday morning, I checked my phone again. Still no text from Katie.

I hadn't talked to her since practice on Thursday night. She'd missed school yesterday because she'd gone with her mom to Chicago for the weekend. She hadn't texted me at all. *Is she still mad about the Avery thing?* I wondered.

I sent her another quick message and then headed out to my backyard gym. That's what I call our yard when I pull my mats and practice beam out there. I did some stretches and then stepped onto my beam to practice handstands.

I spread my fingers wide like Avery had taught me. But that only reminded me that Avery had kept her distance all morning at the gym. Was she still mad, too?

Ding!

I fell out of my handstand and grabbed my phone. Katie had sent a photo of a Ferris wheel. *At Navy Pier in Chicago,* she texted. *You doing anything fun?*

Just practicing gymnastics, I wrote back—too quickly.

Then I remembered that Katie didn't think of gymnastics as "fun" anymore.

I waited for her response, but it never came.

When Jack burst through the back door saying it was time to carve pumpkins, I shook my head. "Not right now," I said.

Jack shrugged. "I'm not waiting," he said as he darted back into the house.

I stepped onto my mat and tried to slide down into the splits. But everything felt tight today—I couldn't make it to the mat.

McKenna would know how to help, I thought sadly. She always had the perfect stretches and drills to get me where I needed to be.

But McKenna wasn't here. And Katie was gone all weekend.

I was on my own.

By Tuesday night, it felt like Katie and I were back to good. She hadn't mentioned the Avery thing at school yesterday, so I'd stayed quiet about it too. But we were *both* hoping McKenna would be back at practice tonight.

The minute Mom dropped us off at Aberg's, we raced into the gym. It had been almost a week since McKenna's grandma's surgery. Wouldn't she be better by now?

I spotted Sawyer talking with Avery. The tips of Sawyer's hair were dyed bright pink, as if she'd needed a fresh start after Thursday's practice. But McKenna was nowhere to be seen.

"Ugh," whispered Katie when she saw Avery. "I don't think I can take any more Avery."

My chest tightened. *Here we go again,* I thought to myself. Things were only getting worse with Katie and Avery, especially without McKenna here. *What would McKenna do?* I wondered.

She would have reminded Avery in her own gentle way that Katie didn't need another coach—she already had two. *Except she doesn't anymore,* I realized sadly. Sawyer was doing her best to help us, but would it be enough?

"All right, girls," Sawyer said as we sat down. "This will be your only practice this week. The gym is closed Thursday so you can enjoy Halloween." Sawyer smiled, as if skipping practice was great news.

"Wait, what?" said Avery. "So we only have"—she held up her fingers one by one—"three more practices before our meet?" Avery was counting down to November 9, just like I was.

Katie nudged my leg and whispered, "Two days till Team Palomino goes trick-or-treating!" Katie wasn't thinking about the meet at all.

Avery shook her head. "We're not ready for this meet."

As soon as floor practice started, I knew Avery was right. I couldn't connect my roundoff to my back handspring. I had to stop after my roundoff before I could even think about launching into my handspring.

During beam, Emilia kept falling off. She threw out her hands and cried, "What is *happening*? I'm a mess!"

And during bar practice, Avery jumped toward the high bar and *missed*. I'd seen her peel off the bar before, her hands slipping. But I'd never seen her miss entirely.

When she landed on the mat, Sawyer hurried over and asked if she was all right. Avery nodded, but I could tell she wasn't. And if Avery was intense before, she only dialed it up a notch after her fall.

When we moved to vault, Avery started coaching Grace. "You have to practice saluting," Avery told her, "so you don't forget at the meet."

Grace, who had already started down the runway, turned around and walked back. She saluted Avery and then took off running again toward the thick mat the Silver team used as a vault.

A shadow passed over Katie's face on her way to the runway. She whispered to me, "I'm not saluting her. She's not a judge."

"I know," I said. "She's just . . ." I didn't finish the thought. Pointing out that Avery was trying to be helpful was *not* helping things between me and Katie.

As soon as Grace rolled off the mat, Avery was ready with a barrage of tips. "Point your toes," she called. "Keep your body tight. It's got to be tighter than that when you're in front of judges."

Grace's face fell.

Katie saw that her teammate was discouraged. "Good vault, Grace," Katie yelled, shooting Avery an annoyed look.

As Katie stepped onto the runway, I heard Avery say, "Remember to salute the judges, Katie."

Uh-oh. Katie's expression instantly changed from irritation to anger.

"I will *not* salute you," she snapped at Avery. "You're not a judge, and you're not our coach. Grace doesn't need you telling her what she's doing wrong, and I don't either. So just *stop*!"

Avery's jaw hung slack, as if she'd just been slapped.

"Girls, let's focus on our own skills," said Sawyer, trying to smooth things over. But it was like trying to frost a warm, crumbly cake.

"The meet is in a week and a half!" said Avery. "If things keep going like this, we're not going to medal at all. Our team won't even place."

"Is that all you care about?" Katie growled. "Medals and scores and *placing*," she said, making air quotes.

Avery scrunched up her face in confusion. "I do care

about medals and scores and placing."

"Well, I think you're way too competitive," said Katie.

Sawyer looked from Katie to Avery as if she were watching a tennis match. McKenna would have known what to do, but Sawyer clearly didn't.

Avery crossed her arms. "Why did you even join Aberg's?" she asked Katie. "Was it just to spend time with Lila? Because this is a competitive team. If you're *not* going to be competitive, then you'll just drag the rest of us down."

"Avery!" Emilia gasped. "You don't have to be mean."

"I'm not trying to be mean," Avery said. "But I do want to win. That's what a competitive team is all about."

Katie's cheeks turned pink. I could tell that Avery's words had stung. "I think what Avery is saying is—" I began.

Katie whirled to face me, hurt flickering across her face. "I can't believe you're taking her side!" Her dark eyes flashed. "You know what, Lila? Avery isn't the only one here who's too competitive. You're becoming *exactly* the same way."

Katie stormed over to the bench, grabbed her jacket and bag, and left the gym. I saw her fumbling with her phone. Was she calling her mom for a ride home? My stomach squeezed.

"Girls, let's take a break," Sawyer said wearily.

Instead of heading to the bench, I raced to the bathroom.

Hot tears welled in my eyes. I tried to hold them in as
I splashed cold water on my face, but I could still taste
their salty sting.

On Wednesday morning, I texted Katie to make sure we
were still biking to school together. I was already pedaling
toward her house when I got her response.

No. Mom is driving me.

The words blurred as I took a shaky breath.

I turned my bike around in a driveway, stopping to wait
for a woman walking a little dog in a sweater. I shivered,
suddenly feeling the cold in the air.

When I got to school, I hurried into our fifth-grade
classroom. Katie was there, sitting next to our friend
Piper. I tried to catch Katie's eye, but she wouldn't look
up—not even when I slid into my desk in the pod next
to hers.

When the loudspeaker crackled, Ms. Wood called us
to attention for daily announcements. Principal Welnetz's
voice came on reminding us that tomorrow was Halloween.
"Let's show some spirit and dress up!" he said.

I shot Katie a hopeful glance, but she avoided my eyes. It
was like an imaginary wall stood between us. All day long,
I tried to climb over it, but I couldn't.

After school, I did the only thing I could think of. Katie

wouldn't talk to me in person, but she had answered my last text. So I tried again.

Are we wearing our Hollyhock costume tomorrow? I texted.

I was almost home by the time she texted back.

No, she wrote. *I don't think so.*

My heart sank.

Dad was stringing orange and purple lights along the porch rail when I biked into the driveway. "What do you think?" he asked, showing off the creepy plastic skeleton he'd pulled out of the attic too.

I gave him a thumbs-up, but I couldn't speak. I pushed my way into the house, wishing I could just crawl into bed.

Tomorrow was Halloween and I had the best costume ever. But how could I be a palomino without my pal—my other half?

Trick or Treat
Chapter 12

Knock, knock!"

Jack burst into my room Thursday night wearing an eye patch and a red bandanna around his head. He had a sword made out of cardboard and tinfoil, and his riding boots pulled on over a pair of tights.

"Who's there?" I mumbled.

"Turner."

"Turner who?"

"Turner round. There's a pirate in your room!"

"Good one," I said, but I couldn't muster up a smile.

"Why aren't you dressed?" he asked. "Where's your horse costume?"

I shrugged. "I don't think I'm going this year," I said.

Jack pulled up his eye patch so he could look at me in disbelief—with both eyes. "Why not?" he said. "What about the candy?"

I shrugged again.

Jack must have been really worried about me, because he ran out of the room calling for Dad.

When Dad came in, Jack trailed behind him. "No costume?" said Dad.

I shook my head. "Katie can't go this year." I couldn't bring myself to say that Katie didn't *want* to go, at least not with me. She had shown up at school dressed as a ballerina, a tutu pulled over one of her gymnastics leos. So maybe she was already out there, trick-or-treating with someone else.

Dad sank onto the bed beside me. He's a psychologist, so he's a pretty good listener. But I didn't feel like talking.

"I'm sorry Katie can't go," said Dad. "But I think you should still go, don't you?"

I shook my head. "I can't be a horse without Katie."

Dad glanced over his shoulder. "Jack, do you want to share Katie's costume?"

Jack's brow furrowed. "No!" he said. "I already learned my pirate jokes. Besides, I don't want to be half a horse."

Dad smiled. "Fair enough," he said, turning back to me. "Do you want *me* to be your other half?"

I shook my head again. "Thanks, but I think you're too tall."

Dad nodded. "Probably true." He straightened up. "Well, here's the deal. Your mom is working tonight, so one of us needs to go with Jack, and one of us needs to stay home to hand out candy. I'm thinking you'll have a lot more fun trick-or-treating."

"Fine," I sighed, pushing myself off the bed. I didn't want to go, but I didn't want to answer the door all night either.

Twenty minutes later, Jack and I were traipsing through wet leaves. Rain drizzled down, which matched my mood perfectly. Instead of dressing as my favorite horse with Katie, I was dressed in last year's cat costume. When I wiped the raindrops off my face, I didn't even care if the rain smeared my cat whiskers.

After one trip around the block, our candy bags were filling up, and I was ready to be done. As Jack hurried up the sidewalk to yet another house, I hung back. Then I heard a familiar voice coming my way.

"Do you want my chocolate?" someone said. "I'll take your sour stuff!"

It was Katie, dressed like a witch. But she wasn't talking to me. She was talking to Piper, who walked beside her—in a matching witch costume.

My chest heaved.

When Katie saw me, something caught in my throat. My eyes burned with tears, and I knew I had to get out of there—fast.

I turned my back on Katie and sprinted up the sidewalk. As soon as Jack had his candy, I grabbed his hand and cut back across the lawn toward home. Tears spilled off my chin, mingling with raindrops.

"Slow down!" Jack cried. "My candy is spilling!"

But I couldn't stop. I couldn't look at Katie all dressed up, enjoying our favorite tradition with *someone else.*

When I got home from school on Friday, I went straight to my room and slammed the door. My trick-or-treat bag slipped off the doorknob, spilling fruit snacks and sour candies onto the floor. If Katie had been with me last night, we would have done a candy swap. She would have taken the sour candy and given me her candy bars. But Katie hadn't been with me.

I didn't eat any candy, but I still had a sour taste in my mouth.

"Knock, knock." It wasn't Jack this time. It was Mom. "Can I come in?"

"Yes," I said with a sigh.

Mom came in and sat on the bed beside me. "Nice braids."

I had worn French braids today, hoping Katie would have worn hers too. It was tradition. But Katie had worn a ponytail, and she had avoided me all day.

"Katie won't talk to me," I blurted, before Mom could even ask. "She thinks I'm being too competitive in gymnastics. But I just want to do well! We used to like all the same things, but now I don't even think she likes gymnastics anymore. Everything is changing."

I took a ragged breath and nestled my head against Mom.

She stroked my hair and was silent for a moment. Then she said, "One of the hardest things about having a best friend is letting each other change and grow. You're not always going to love the same things. And that's okay."

I bit my lip. "But what if . . . we grow apart?" I said. My stomach twisted at the thought of not having Katie as my best friend. I didn't think I could bear it.

Mom stroked my head again. "You know what I think?" she said.

She waited until I looked up.

"I think friendships are like braids." She lifted one of my braids so that I could see it, and then began tracing the woven strands with her finger. "See how the strands of hair separate and then come back together?"

I nodded.

"That's how good friendships are," said Mom. "You and Katie might separate or drift apart sometimes, but I think you'll always find your way back to each other."

I stared at that braid for a while, hoping Mom was right. "But how can I bring us back together?" I asked.

Mom tilted her head so that she could see my face. "You said you don't always enjoy the same things anymore," she said. "So what does Katie enjoy now?"

"Goats," was the first thing that came to mind. "She's totally and completely obsessed with a baby goat named Buttons. Let me show you."

I grabbed my phone and pulled up the Honeycrisp Hill website. I clicked on the latest Buttons video, which Mrs. Benson had just posted. Mom and I laughed as the little white goat bounded across the pen. Buttons was getting so big!

Then Mrs. Benson said something that made my heart leap. "Tomorrow is a big day for Buttons! She's going to be reunited with her siblings in the morning. Be sure to check back for that reunion video tomorrow."

I dropped my phone and jumped up off my bed. "Mom," I said. "We have to go. Katie *can't* say no to that!"

Mom cocked her head. "Tomorrow morning? Jack has a riding lesson, so we're heading to Honeycrisp Hill anyway. But you have gymnastics."

I slumped back down on the bed. "Yes. And the meet is only a week away." I swallowed hard, thinking about how badly I wanted to do well at that meet. But there was something else I wanted even more.

I parked my bike on Katie's porch and I rang the doorbell. When Katie answered the door, she looked surprised to see me.

I started talking fast, before she could turn away. "Buttons is going to be reunited with her siblings tomorrow morning," I said. "Will you come with me? My mom would drive us, but . . . I know you have dance lessons."

One emotion after another raced across Katie's face: excitement, worry, and then confusion. "But you have gymnastics, and the meet is only a week away."

I nodded. "I can skip one Saturday morning. I need to practice for the meet, but . . . this is more important."

Katie's face softened into a smile. "Let me ask my mom."

She didn't invite me to come inside. I stood outside the screen door as she disappeared into the house.

Yeowl!

Harry batted at the door from inside. He wanted out just as much as I wanted in.

When Katie came back, she was grinning from ear to ear. *Yes!*

We were going to see Buttons reunited with her sister and brother tomorrow. And maybe that would help me and Katie find our way back to each other too.

Buddies and Buttons
Chapter 13

B etter stand back, girls," said Mr. Benson. He held a squirming Buttons in his arms and was about to put her in the pen with Olive and Pepper. She bleated excitedly.

"Ready?" Mr. Benson asked his wife, who held up her phone to take the video.

"Ready!" she said. "Let's not keep Buttons waiting another minute."

As soon as Buttons set foot in the pen, Olive and Pepper bounded over to greet her. They welcomed her with a chorus of bleats, and soon the three kids were jumping joyfully, kicking out their back legs and climbing over one another.

"Oh, she's so happy," said Katie. "Look at her tail go!"

"Look how big Buttons has gotten," said Mrs. Benson. "She's down to only one bottle of milk a day, but she's been eating enough goat feed lately to catch up to her sister and brother."

Mom smiled. "I guess a little separation was good for her," she said. "It helped her grow." She glanced my way and winked.

"But now they're all back together," said Katie. "And it's about time."

Mrs. Benson let Katie and me step into the pen with the goats, and soon they were scampering all over us, too.

When Jack wanted to join us, Mr. Benson told him it was time for his lesson. "Want to help me saddle up Joker?"

Jack sprinted to the barn, with Mr. Benson and Mom following. When Mrs. Benson went down to the farmhouse to get some goat feed, Katie and I sat together in awkward silence.

There was so much I wanted to say to her. But how could I even begin?

"Knock, knock," I finally said.

Katie shot me a weird look, but she played along. "Who's there?"

"Goat," I said.

"Goat who?"

"Goat to the barn door to find out," I said.

Katie paused, letting the punch line sink in. "That was so dumb," she groaned, but then she started giggling.

Which made me laugh.

Which made Katie laugh harder.

Pretty soon, I was laughing so hard that my stomach hurt. Katie's laughter came in silent waves. When she finally stopped, we both had tears rolling down our cheeks.

We watched the goats, who were still nosing at each other playfully. "I'm sorry we haven't had much fun together lately," I said, forcing the words out. "I thought trick-or-treating—"

"I'm sorry about that," Katie interrupted. "I'm sorry I bailed on Team Palomino."

My stomach clenched. The memory of seeing Katie trick-or-treating with Piper still hurt.

"As soon as I saw you that night, I wished I were with you," said Katie. "I should have been with you." She looked at me, her face so sad and sorry that I knew she meant it.

"We'll be together next year," I told her.

Katie smiled gratefully.

Then I took a deep breath. "I know I've gotten more

serious at gymnastics," I said, struggling to find the right words. "I'm just trying to keep getting better."

When Katie faced me, her eyes were earnest. "You *are* getting better," she said. "You did really well at the mock meet. You've gotten a lot of skills since you joined Aberg's."

Heat rushed to my cheeks at the compliment. "I've been working really hard," I acknowledged, "but I think I did so well at the mock meet because I was nervous. I had all that extra energy!" I hesitated and then added, "But I know it wasn't the same for you. I know gymnastics isn't all that fun for you anymore."

Katie sighed and stretched her legs out in front of her. "I still like gymnastics," she admitted. "I really like having McKenna as a coach. But I really, really don't like competing. If I'm scared or nervous, I can't do *anything* right."

When Katie's shoulders slumped, I didn't know what to say. I knew how to help Hollyhock when she got spooked or scared, but I didn't know how to help my best friend.

"I guess everybody's different," I said with a shrug. "You and Emilia both get really nervous before meets. McKenna says that's normal."

"But you and Avery don't," said Katie.

I tensed up at the mention of Avery's name. There was something else I had to say to Katie.

"I'm sorry," I began carefully, "if you thought I was taking Avery's side. She's a good gymnast and she tries to give good tips, even if we don't always want them. But *you're* my best friend. I'll always, always, always have your back."

"Thanks," Katie said, smiling sadly. "It is kinda my fault that Avery got so intense. I mean, I did spill McKenna's secret about leaving." Katie picked at a piece of straw. "And Avery was right about why I joined Aberg's. I joined to spend time with you. But if I'm dragging down the team, especially at meets, maybe I should quit."

"You're not dragging down the team!" I said, putting my arm around Katie. "You're *part* of the team. Besides, we've only had one meet. Give yourself another chance."

Katie leaned into my hug. "I wish McKenna was here. She was going to come up with ways to help me and Emilia feel less nervous, remember?"

I nodded. McKenna would know how to help Katie, just like she always knew how to help me. "What would McKenna do?" I wondered aloud. It was the question I'd been asking myself ever since she'd left.

"She'd probably tell me to sing my floor music at the top of my lungs before the meet," Katie said. "So I'd feel less nervous."

"Ooh, and she'd want us to dance too," I said, remembering how we'd all jammed out in McKenna's car. "And wear matching hairdos, like she used to do with her sisters."

"Yes!" said Katie. "And she'd let us wear purple nail polish all week, right up until the day of the meet. Go, Team Purple!"

"Or purple buddy tape," I said, remembering how she'd taped my toe to the one next to it. "To remind us that we're stronger together."

"Definitely," said Katie. She glanced at me. When she grinned, I knew we were on to something.

"I think we need a sleepover," I said. "So we can keep thinking up ways to make the next meet more fun."

I was relieved when Katie said, "Yes. Go, Team Purple!"

It seemed like Katie and I were finding our way back together, just like Mom had said we would. Could we pull our team back together before the meet too?

We had seven days to find out.

Stronger Together

Chapter 14

I don't get it," said Avery, her forehead wrinkling.

"It's a star made out of tape," I said, holding up one of the purple stars Katie and I had made over the weekend. "We made one for each of you to hang on your gym bags."

It was Tuesday night, and Katie and I had arrived at the gym early to share our ideas with Sawyer for making our team stronger. Sawyer had been all ears.

"Tell the team why you made them," Sawyer said with a smile.

"McKenna used athletic tape to wrap my toes together," I explained. "She called it 'buddy tape,' because my toes would be stronger when wrapped together. So Katie and I made these to remind everyone that we're stronger together too. We're a team."

"Team Purple!" Katie added. "Oh, and it's a star because McKenna keeps a star necklace from her grandma to remember that her grandma is always cheering her on. These stars can remind us that McKenna is cheering us on, too, even if she can't be here."

"I love it," said Emilia, leaning forward to choose a star.

Grace took one too, but Avery still looked confused.

"Our team has kind of been struggling, hasn't it?" said Sawyer. "Katie and Lila reminded me this morning that we need to have more fun."

"But the meet is four days away!" said Avery. "We don't have time—"

I interrupted Avery. "Having fun *will* help us get ready for the meet," I explained. "Every gymnast is different. Some gymnasts get really nervous before a meet, and having fun helps them relax and actually do better."
I didn't name Katie or Emilia, but they both flashed me grateful smiles.

Avery didn't look so sure about that, but when Sawyer said "Ready to work?" the rest of us chimed in with an extra loud "Ready to fly!"

During floor practice, I reminded Katie of our plan. She played her floor music one time through without doing the skills. Instead, we sang the lyrics—and added the dance moves we'd made up over the weekend.

"What … is … happening?" Emilia asked as she watched us dance.

Katie answered her in song. "Throw away your fears and take a chance. All we gotta do is dance, dance, dance!"

That was all the invitation Emilia needed. She ran onto the mat and joined us, busting out a few silly moves.

Sawyer grinned and waved Grace over to the mat. But Avery hung back. She worked on handstands in the corner.

When the music ended and Katie ran through her actual routine, she soared. I could see her lips moving, as if she were still singing those lyrics. And when she struck her final pose, she was smiling.

Avery noticed too—she raised her eyebrows as Katie saluted Sawyer and stepped off the mat. *Will Avery get it now?* I wondered. *Does she understand why we need to have more fun?*

Katie's smile gave me the confidence to tackle my roundoff back handspring on the spring floor instead of the tumble tramp.

"Do you need a spot?" asked Sawyer.

"Maybe," I acknowledged.

I went into my roundoff strong, but I still couldn't connect the skills—even with Sawyer's help. The pause between the two was just too long.

I sighed as I came out of my handspring, but Katie was right there with a smile. "You've got this," she said. "Go, Team Purple!"

"Thanks," I said, happy to see Katie so happy. But I needed help with my tumbling—and I knew who to ask.

When Katie moved on to a stacked mat to practice leaps, I waved Avery over. "Do you have any tips?" I asked. "For connecting my roundoff and back handspring?"

Avery chewed her lip. She glanced in Katie's direction and said, "I probably shouldn't give advice anymore."

"It's okay," I said quickly. "I'm asking for it. I really need it."

Avery's face relaxed into a smile. "Okay," she said, "Let me think. Maybe try talking yourself through it, like to the beats of each move. Say the words in your head: *Round. Off. To. Back. Hand. Spring.* Then try to make your pause—on the word *to*—shorter and shorter."

I nodded and tried again, talking myself through every step. Somehow, keeping my mind busy made me worry less about connecting the skills. I paused a little too long on the word *to*, but that was okay. Thanks to Avery, at least I had a plan.

"Hold still," I told Avery as I finished her second braid. The woven strands of her red hair shone under the bright fluorescent lights of the restroom.

Avery had finally agreed to let me do her hair for the meet, and all of us from Aberg's Gym were wearing matching purple ribbons. "Team Purple," I announced as we looked in the mirror.

"Hair by Lila," Katie added.

Sawyer's hair wasn't long enough to braid, but she had dyed the tips purple, just for the meet today. She grinned at us in the mirror. "Ready to work?"

"Ready to fly!" we cheered.

When I closed my duffel, the purple star I'd made dangled from the zipper pull. I touched the star for good luck, reminding myself that McKenna was cheering us on—even if she couldn't be here.

As soon as we stepped into the hall, the chaos of the meet hit us. Teams of girls streamed past, sparkling in their competition leos. Tables and racks were filled with leotards, pop-its, plush stuffies, and other good-luck gear. Balloons arched over the doorways to the gym.

When we stepped inside, music blared from every corner. Girls were practicing their floor routines, all the songs blending into one. Coaches sipped coffee from thermoses, and parents sat on benches by the beams, bars, and mats. Vault was set up along the back of the gym, just beneath two big scoreboards.

Katie started hiccupping, her face pale.

"No, no, no," I said, throwing my arm over her shoulder. "We've got this!" But my own stomach fluttered. I was nercited, but this morning I felt more *nervous* than excited. We were a long way from the comfort of Aberg's Gym.

"Do we need music?" I asked, holding up my phone.

Emilia nodded. "Definitely."

We had all downloaded Katie's floor music—it was our team song now. After Sawyer showed us where to store our backpacks and jackets, I hit play.

"C'mon, Katie," I said. "Show us your stuff."

She swayed a little to the music, and then a little more. Pretty soon her cheeks were pink again and she was jamming out. The team warming up next to us cast curious looks our way, but we didn't care. Team Purple was doing its own kind of warm-up.

When I heard someone singing behind me, I turned to find Avery bobbing her head.

"Avery," I said, busting her. "You know the words!"

She froze for a second, then laughed. "I can't help it!" she said. "You all played that song like a hundred times this week." She glanced at Katie and added, "It's a pretty good song."

Katie grinned at Avery for probably the first time ever, and then finished the song with a dramatic pose. She was out of breath as she flopped onto the mat next to me. Then she sank into silence again. I wished we could play Katie's song all morning long, booming it out over the speaker system. But at least the Silver team was competing first. That meant the rest of us could cheer on Katie and Grace.

If I saw Katie freaking out, I was going to flash one of my goofiest faces from the sidelines. If I could keep her laughing, I knew she'd be all right.

I scanned the crowd looking for Mom and Dad. I was about to compete on floor, and I needed all the support I could get. Jack waved, Mom blew me a kiss, and Dad pumped his fist in the air. "Go get 'em!" he mouthed.

Katie waved, too, from her spot on the floor. She looked so relaxed now that her events were over. I still couldn't believe how well she'd done. I'd only had to make a silly face at her *once*—right before beam, when she was worried she'd fall off. We all hummed her song between events and kept her calm so she wouldn't get the hiccups.

But now it was my turn.

Sawyer gave me a high five as I stepped to the mat. I couldn't help wishing it were McKenna by my side. *What would McKenna do?* I wondered again. She would say, "You've got this." She would remind me that the adrenaline, that nervousness I was feeling, would only make me faster and stronger. And she would say, "Ready to work?"

"Ready to fly," I murmured as I saluted the judges. When my music started, my body moved all on its own. I launched into my first dance pass, turning on the ball of my foot, touching my shoulders, and extending my arms. I sashayed to the corner and counted off my heel taps. At the opposite corner, I counted off *one, two, three, four.*

Then it was time.

I lined up for my tumbling pass, feeling a surge of energy. I sprinted into my roundoff, saying the moves in my head: *Round. Off. To . . .*

On the word *to,* I was already launching into my back handspring. I didn't need a pause. I couldn't have paused even if I'd wanted to!

The momentum from the roundoff helped me push through my toes and launch skyward, swinging my arms overhead. The power from my legs drove me backward until my palms hit the floor. Then my legs snapped down, just the way McKenna had taught me.

When I landed, I instantly popped back up, releasing

all the energy that had carried me through the pass. I took a step backward, but I raised my arms overhead proudly. It was the best roundoff back handspring I had ever done.

I glided through my next dance pass and then did my front walkover into a sit—the move McKenna had chosen just for me, because of my flexibility. I got back up and pulled off two more tumbling moves, easily sailing through my aerial cartwheel.

Then I soared through my leap pass, so high off the mat that I thought I'd never come back down.

When the song ended, I struck a final pose, grinning ear to ear as I tried to catch my breath.

Salute the judges! I could almost hear Avery say. I gave my final salute and then jogged off the mat.

My teammates were calling my name, ready to celebrate with me. But I had to see my score. Which scoreboard would it pop up on? I looked for Sawyer to help me figure it out.

Then I saw someone else jogging toward me. Someone with a caramel-colored bun and a warm smile.

McKenna.

Something cracked in my chest and then I was crying and laughing all at the same time. "You're here!" I exclaimed as she pulled me into a hug.

McKenna squeezed me tight and said, "I wouldn't have missed it. I'm so sorry I'm late."

I buried my face in McKenna's shoulder for a few

seconds, overwhelmed with relief and happiness. Then I wiped my face and pulled away. "Is your grandma okay?" I asked.

McKenna smiled and nodded. "She's getting there. She was feeling well enough yesterday to order me back to Minnesota so that I could cheer on my favorite gymnasts. Speaking of which"—she turned me around to face the scoreboard—"let's see how you did."

Together, we watched and waited. I held my breath until I saw my name. And then my score.

Lila Monetti   9.425

When McKenna whooped and squeezed my shoulder, I felt like I'd scored a perfect 10.

"I did it," I whispered. I'd gotten my roundoff back handspring. I'd scored almost a whole point more than I had in floor at the mock meet! And I'd made my favorite coach proud.

"Gymnasts salute!"

As cameras flashed, I smiled and raised my arms in the air. I held my pose long enough for Mom to get a picture. Then I hopped off the podium, my medals jangling.

When Katie gave me a high five, her medals jingled too. She had made the podium on floor and bars! She had just as many medals around her neck as Grace this time, and her cheeks were pink with excitement.

We were sitting on the floor in front of the podium, clustered around McKenna. Sawyer seemed relieved to have our head coach back too. She was smiling ear to ear.

"Second place on floor and third place on bars?" McKenna whispered to me. "That's amazing!"

"I didn't think I could do it without you," I confessed.

She looked me straight in the eye. "I *knew* you could," she said. "You don't need me to motivate you. You're doing it for yourself now. You're following your heart." She tapped my chest, just above my medals. "You're following your passion."

I nodded. I'd never felt so passionate about gymnastics before.

When Katie giggled about something with Emilia, I glanced at my best friend. She was having fun again. *Finally.* I knew we wouldn't always love the same things. But I wasn't worried about growing apart anymore.

Good friends always find their way back to each other, I thought to myself.

I tugged on the end of Katie's braid and gave her a smile.

MEET COACH MCKENNA

Since McKenna's been such a big part of my gymnastics journey, I asked her if I could interview her. Here's what I learned.

WHERE DID YOU GROW UP?
Seattle, Washington

WHY DID YOU MOVE TO MINNESOTA?
I came here for college. I also started coaching gymnastics, which is a lot of fun.

HOW LONG HAVE YOU BEEN DOING GYMNASTICS?
Nineteen years. I started at Shooting Star Gymnastics when I was three years old, and I trained there until I moved to Minnesota.

WHEN DID YOU BEGIN COMPETING?
When I was ten years old, I moved to level four in gymnastics and started working on the skills I would need to join the competitive team. We had six months to train, and there were only two spots open. After a LOT of work, I made the team!

McKenna, age 10, on the uneven bars

128

Josie rode a sweet horse named Pumpkin.

WHEN DID YOU START WORKING WITH HORSES?

When I was ten. A friend of mine—Josie—uses a wheelchair and wanted to learn how to ride. She was going to a horseback riding center for people with disabilities called Hearts and Horses. Josie was nervous, so she asked me to come along to support her. I thought the center was awesome. They needed volunteers, so I signed up.

WHAT DO YOU LIKE MOST ABOUT COACHING?

I like working with young athletes, and coaching has given me a new way to appreciate the sport.

SURPRISE!

MCKENNA BROOKS WAS THE 2012 GIRL OF THE YEAR!

Teamwork

You've seen the movie: The team is a bunch of misfits and newbies who bump into one another at every turn. Slowly they get better, and at the end—big hurray!—they bring home the trophy.

In real life, teammates don't go from chumps to champs in two hours. Teamwork takes time.

To learn more about teamwork and solo sports, check out *A Smart Girls Guide: Sports and Fitness.*

That happens at practices. Practices are a time to improve your skills, learn how to work with teammates, and get to know one another. The more comfortable you feel with your teammates, the easier it is to play as one smooth machine.

How well do you know your teammates? Look at the girl next to you at practice. Who's her favorite pro athlete? What's her dog's name? If you don't know, find out!

Once you and your teammates become friends, you develop a powerful closeness called *esprit de corps* (es-PREE deh KOR). It's the spirit that makes working hard fun and that binds you together *closerthanthis!*

Get-to-know-you games

To strengthen the bonds with your teammates, play these games before practice, on the way to an event, or even while you wait for your ride home.

Two truths and a tale

Stand in a circle. Each girl makes three statements about herself—two that are true and one that's an untrue "tale." The girl to her left guesses which statement is the tale. Then it's her turn. By the end, you'll know much more about your teammates and their imaginations!

> I have a cat named Sandy Claws.

> My great-grandma played professional baseball.

> I rode in a submarine.

Fun facts

To play, you need a bag of colored items, such as large beads or candies. Stand in a circle. Without explaining the rules, have each girl grab a handful from the bag. Surprise!—the number of beads or candies she grabs equals the number of fun facts she has to share about herself. If you like, make each color a different subject. For example:

pets or favorite animals

friends

family

school

sports

10 ways to be a leader

Teams are made up of all kinds of people: younger and older kids, speed demons and slow-but-steadies, girls with experience and girls with new passion. Everyone has something to contribute.

The best athletes know that being part of the team is more important than being the star of the show. They also know that the most talented athlete isn't the only leader on the team. There are other ways to show award-winning behavior. Challenge yourself—can you model at least five of these all-star actions at every practice?

Support

Help other girls by sharing what you know—without making them feel dumb. If you notice a teammate is struggling with something, such as a family or school matter, ask if she would like to talk.

Encourage

Praise other girls out loud—in front of the team—for things they do well. Prove that this is a team whose members support one another.

Make extra effort

Give it all you've got at practice, and truly pay attention to your coach. Always be ready to run one more lap.

Raise the bar

Challenge teammates in a fun and friendly way. If the coach yells, "Eight push-ups!" smile at the girl next to you and say, "I bet we can do ten. Let's try!"

Be a tough cookie

When you fall down, don't crumble. Bounce back up! If you make a mistake, move on instead of sweating it. Stay positive under pressure and mentally tough under stress. You'll empower others to do the same.

Be a storm chaser

Do you see black clouds of negativity forming? Take action! If teammates are complaining, focus on solutions instead of joining in. Show that "can't-do" attitudes have no place here.

Present with pride

Be a good representative of your team, your sport, and yourself. Be polite. Say please and thank you. Participate in class. Put down your phone and be interested in other people. Play with younger kids. Be someone others look up to—and someone you look up to!

Be smart

Show that academics matter. At weekend tourneys and meets, don't be afraid to study between events. If the team has a long bus ride, crack open a book.

Connect

Make an effort to get to know *all* your teammates. Talk and share with the girls who aren't already your friends. Building relationships helps you care about one another. When you care, you work harder for each other in the game.

Energize

Keep the team's spirits high with a smile and enthusiasm. Both are infectious!

It's important to have your own goals, but remember—you need your team in order to reach those goals! You're in this together.

Reader Questions

- Lila says riding Hollyhock helped her get over her fear of falling off the high bar at gymnastics. Why do you think horseback riding would make Lila less nervous about falling?

- Why does Lila feel guilty when she discovers that Katie painted her bedroom walls?

- What does McKenna mean when she says, "Different personalities make for a more balanced team"?

- Some of the gymnasts get nervous at the meet. Lila feels a burst of energy that fuels her routine. Katie gets the hiccups. Emilia talks a lot. What do you do when you feel nervous? How do you calm your nerves?

- Avery tells Katie, "This is a competitive team. If you're not going to be competitive, then you'll just drag the rest of us down." Do you think Avery was being mean? Why or why not?

- Lila misses a gymnastics practice so that she and Katie can see Buttons reunited with her siblings. What are some other ways Lila supports Katie's interests? How does Katie support Lila?

- Lila reminds her teammates, "We're stronger together." How do they work together during the second meet? How do their actions impact Lila? How do they impact Katie?

About the
Author, Illustrator, and Advisers

Erin Falligant took horseback riding lessons when she was a girl, just like Lila. But while Lila dreams of becoming a competitive gymnast, Erin dreamed of becoming an author—long before she wrote her first book. She has now written more than forty books for children, including contemporary fiction, historical fiction, advice books, and picture books. She has a master's degree in child clinical psychology and writes from her home in Madison, Wisconsin.

Vivienne To is an illustrator and concept artist. She has worked in the art department for several animated feature films, and her illustrations have been featured on many book covers and in many picture books. Vivienne lives in Wellington, New Zealand. When she isn't drawing, she can be found knitting on the couch, watching cute dogs at the local park, or getting lost in a good book.

Sarah Nelson is the business manager and head competitive gymnastics coach at Madtown Twisters Gymnastics. She has coached gymnasts of all levels—from the preschool level all the way up to future collegiate athletes. She is also a nationally ranked gymnastics official and judges competitions all over the United States.

Ted Marthe is the co-owner of Hoofbeat Ridge Camps. He has directed both private and agency camps. Ted is the former executive director of the Horsemanship Safety Association, an organization dedicated to certifying horseback riding instructors and helping camps run safe horsemanship programs.

Visit **americangirl.com/play**
to discover more about Lila's world.

Look for bestselling books from
American Girl online and in stores.

Published by American Girl Publishing

24 25 26 27 28 29 30 QP 10 9 8 7 6 5 4 3 2 1

This book is a work of fiction. Any similarity to real persons, living or
dead, is coincidental and not intended by American Girl. References
to real events, people, or places are used fictitiously. Other names,
characters, places, and incidents are the products of imagination.

Written by Erin Falligant
Cover image and illustrations by Vivienne To
Book design by Gretchen Becker

Cataloging-in-Publication Data available from the Library of Congress

americangirl.com/service

Not all services are available in all countries.